"I am making a Bollywood-style musical. Please tell Mr. Pinocchio that I enjoyed his book very much, and ask him if he would like to invest in my movie."

—Danniel B., Los Angeles, California

"People are sewn into their skins for life."

—Franz K., Prague

"I wish I had written this book."

—Dolly T., Montreal, Canada

"Anyone who has ever had a bad Pinot Noir will relate to this harrowing story."

—Pedro C., New York City

a

million

little

lies

a

million

little

lies

james pinocchio
with **pablo f. fenjves**

ReganBooks
An Imprint of HarperCollins*Publishers*

HarperCollins books may be purchased for educational, business, or sales promotional use. For information please write: Special Markets Department, HarperCollins Publishers Inc., 10 East 53rd Street, New York, NY 10022.

FIRST EDITION

Designed by Sarah Gubkin

Printed on acid-free paper

Library of Congress Cataloging-in-Publication Data has been applied for.

ISBN 10 0-06-117146-8
ISBN 13 978-0-06-117146-8

06 07 08 09 10 WBC/RRD 10 9 8 7 6 5 4 3 2 1

For
My Friend Janos
Bon Vivant Extraordinaire

I had a little Wooden Sailboat

Which I Made Myself

With My Own Two Hands

And some Asshole in High School

Pushed me into a locker

And it broke

Into A Million Little Pieces.

That little sailboat will never sail,

Because it's in A Million Little Pieces

And it can't be fixed.

But Don't Worry About Me:

I'm Sailing Right Along

All the Way to the Bank.

a

million

little

lies

I am five years old again, and I am in ballet class, in a pink tutu, crying like a little girl. I have just been told that I got the lead in *The Red Shoes*. All of my friends are gathered around me, also crying. They are very happy for me. Then I realize that this must be a dream, because I'm a guy, and I never took ballet classes, and I was only in a tutu once in my life, at the age of twenty-four, and that was only after drinking voluminous amounts of cheap Pinot Noir, which explains the tutu but in no way condones it—although I'm not saying it was wrong, per se, and in fact I believe I quite enjoyed myself over the course of the evening (well, *parts* of it, anyway).

Then I find myself flying through outer space and smacking the right side of my head against what appears to be the window of a cab. I open my eyes. It *is* the window of a cab. I look around. I can see the back of the driver's head, swathed in a turban that seems too big for him (or anyone else, for that matter). I feel something heavy pulling at my left earlobe. It really hurts. I reach up and touch it and the pain shoots through me, white-hot. Pain pain pain. I take a deep breath and once again try to identify the source of the pain. My fingers fumble over the object, carefully, gently, like a blind man curling up with a good Braille book, though not exactly. Before long, I come to the conclusion that an old-fashioned combination lock is hanging from my left earlobe, literally piercing the tender flesh. This can't be so, of course, and I wonder whether I'm still dreaming. Perhaps I've been dreaming all along. Perhaps I was in a dream within a dream, and I woke from that first (or second) dream to find myself in yet another dream, which was even deeper than all the dreams that came before it. Perhaps my whole life has been a dream. This makes me think about the nature of reality, objective and otherwise, and I am forced to ask myself what Plato meant about those shadows on the walls of the cave, though I never really understood any of that, and I'm not entirely sure it's even relevant.

Suddenly, with a deafening screech, the cab pulls to an abrupt stop. I am flung clear across the seat again, and the combination lock hits the glass with a loud, theatrical CLANG! It hurts like a motherfucker! I end up sliding to the floor, wedged tight, unable to extricate myself, and frankly unwilling even to make the slightest effort on my own behalf. I hear the driver screaming at me from the front seat, but I can only understand a few words. *Chicken tikka masala, raita, garlic nan.* The words don't really add up to much, but for some reason I feel hungry, and I wonder if I have forgotten to eat. *Again.*

The next thing I know, the driver is getting out of the car. He yanks open the back door and looks down at me, scowling. I notice that he has a long white beard, flecked with gray, and that from this angle, upside down, the turban looks a little like the Leaning Tower of Pizza. (Caps not mine.) He curses in a foreign tongue, or a vague facsimile thereof, then storms off. Now that I have an unobstructed view through the open door, I realize that we are in front of my parents' Park Avenue co-op. I can see the elegant blue canopy from where I'm lying, with the bright white numbers etched across the front. I wonder how the driver knew to bring me here. I wonder who gave him the address. I try to remember where I was last night, but nothing comes back to me. Only the dancing. And the Pinot Noir. And more dancing. Always the dancing.

A moment later, two familiar upside-down faces come into view: Pedro and Raul, the doormen. They have brought the wheelchair. They study the situation with all the somberness of professional movers, deliberating earnestly, and finally get to work. After a few minutes, they manage to drag me from the floor of the cab and into the wheelchair. They do this without any tenderness whatsoever, and I can't say I blame them: They are sick of me.

What the fuck? Pedro says abruptly. He is staring at the left side of my head, grinning his lopsided grin. Pedro is a handsome man, but short. Very short. If he was any shorter, he'd remind me of a trash-compactor, though maybe that's just a word-association thing running through my head: *Short. Compact. Trash.*

Why'd you put a combination lock in your ear?! Pedro says, laughing now. Is that supposed to be cool? You think that makes you Johnny Depp or something? So I was right. It *is* a combination lock. I'm not as blind as all that.

Jimbo, man, you are fucking crazy! You are totally *loco*, *maricón!*

The other guy, Raul, doesn't say anything. He has one of those sad faces. You know the kind: you look at him and you want to cry. Sometimes I think about those two guys, Pedro and Raul, living in Spanish Harlem or wherever the hell they live, and I wonder about their hopes and dreams. But not often. The truth is, I hardly ever think about them. I don't even know if they exist, frankly. They just seem like colorful, cinematic characters, and here they are now, taking me into the opulent lobby, with Raul returning to his post behind the desk, a job he was literally born to (but that's another story), and Pedro wheeling me into the spacious elevator.

So how do you get that fucking thing off? Pedro asks me.

I don't know, I say. I don't even know how the fuck it got there.

Like you don't even know the combination?! he asks, incredulous.

No, I say. I haven't thought that far ahead.

This strikes me as interesting, because almost by default I Am Living in the Now, which seems to be the thing to do lately.

Coño, man! Pedro says, laughing. *Estás jodido!*

We make the rest of the journey in silence.

When we get upstairs, to the penthouse, my mother is waiting. My parents own the whole floor. Pedro rolls me toward her, with the wheels squeaking ominously, like something out of a horror movie, and the place is so endlessly vast that my mother appears to be miles away, literally, figuratively, and—most importantly— *symbolically*.

We finally reach her side and she takes one look at me and begins to cry.

Jimmy, my God! What happened?

I don't remember, Mom.

She's not really my mother, but I call her that anyway. My real mother left when I was two. It didn't really affect me, except for the rest of my life. At this juncture, I would like to mention—parenthetically, but without using the actual parentheses—that I only tell you this to help you understand why I turned out the way I turned out. Maybe you'll be a tad more sympathetic. I wonder if I should mention the Park Avenue co-op? If I left that out, would it be a lie? And I don't want to lie. No. Above all else, there must be no lying. *The truth is what matters. Remember the truth. It is all that matters.*

What is that thing on your earlobe? my mother asks, unable to disguise her horror.

I don't know, Mom. I think it's a combination lock.

It *is* a combination lock. I used to have one just like it on my high school locker.

Maybe it's yours, I say. Maybe you put it there.

My mother begins to cry harder.

Why do you blame me for everything?

I don't blame you for everything. I blame you for *almost* everything. The rest I blame on Dad.

My father shows up. He is one of those wildly successful businessmen who only gets emotional about golf and basketball. But this time, for the first time, he looks genuinely crushed. That really fucks me up. It seems like I've been waiting my whole life to hurt him badly enough to see if he really cares about me, and now that the Great Day is finally here I realize I would have been better off not knowing. I feel awful. I want to cry. I want to die. I want to not be. To. Not. Be.

Consuelo emerges from the kitchen. She is only thirty years old but looks fifty. She has three kids in El Salvador, but she is here in New York, tending to my parents' baser needs. This is as it should be. How many people get a chance to live in Manhattan, the Center of the Universe, in a great co-op, within walking distance of some of the finest wine stores in the Known World? Not many. Consuelo will have wonderful stories to tell her children, if she ever sees them again.

Consuelo also cries, but I don't think she's crying for me. Does anyone really cry for anyone else? Or are they crying for the part of themselves that they see reflected in That Other? For a moment, I wonder if that's what Plato was talking about, though it doesn't feel exactly right, and I realize I will never grasp it and decide I need to let it go. Let. It. Go. If you love something, or even if you don't love it, you should let it go. If it comes back, deal with it. Or not. Your choice.

We're going to help you, son, my father says, his words thick with emotion. Or maybe that's not what he said at all. Maybe he said he was sick of my shit. Maybe he said I was a fucking loser, and that he'd had quite enough, and that I could forget about my Trust Fund, which didn't kick in for another two years, anyway. I don't remember what he said, frankly. I was pretty fucked up. And does it really matter? Does the truth really set you free or was the person who made that up just trying to unearth everyone's deepest, darkest secrets?

I sleep for fourteen hours straight. When I get up, my parents, and my brother, Geppetto, who is three years older than me, and who is already enjoying the benefits of his Trust Fund, are waiting for me in the living room. Every time I see Geppetto I am reminded of his Very Rich and Mind-Bogglingly Insane First Wife, president of the local chapter of the National Rifle Association. I will never understand how my brother managed to drag himself out of the woods with so many bullets in his body.

What's going on? I say.

You're going to Sleepy Hollow, my father says.

No! I say, fighting The Fury inside me. Not Sleepy Hollow! I'll be good! I promise!

I'm sorry, my father says. You need help. The kind of help you need, we can't give you. But we're loaded, so we'll pay for it.

I cried.

Cried. Cried. Cried.

I cried like a little girl.

Cried

Like

A little

Girl

1.

I am crying.

Cry-ing.

Cry cry crying.

Like. A little. Girl.

We are at The Facility, at Sleepy Hollow, New York. It is a sprawling compound for people like me, People Who Drink Too Much Pinot Noir and Dance Dance Dance. Always the Dancing. I drink Pinot Noir. I Dance. I am Garbage.

We are checking in, and we have just been ushered into the white-white office of Lorraine R., one of the in-house psychiatrists. She is forty and attractive in a forty-year-old kind of way, which isn't really all that attractive, come to think of it, especially in our youth-obsessed culture, but I sense there is more to her than meets the eye. I wonder if I detect a slight Viennese accent, and whether her real name is Brunhilde, but it's possible that this is just a figment of my overactive imagination.

You've come to the right place, Lorraine says.

I laugh. I have a big, honking laugh that sounds like the bark of a seal. Or is it a sea lion? I can never get that straight. (Imagine Steve Carell doing that laugh. Or Will Ferrell, if he still has a career.)

Do you find this amusing? Lorraine asks me, but she does it with a tenderness that seems maternal, though not *exactly* maternal, as will become obvious at a later juncture in the story.

No, I say. I just laugh when I'm nervous.

You have nothing to be nervous about, Jimmy. If you behave. We have a lot of rules here, and the one big rule is, *No Dancing*. If you don't dance, and you follow the other rules, of which there are many—didn't I just say that?—you will be fine.

She tells me to say goodbye to my parents, and to my brother, Geppetto, which I do. I do not hug my parents. I can hardly stand touching them. My brother punches me on the shoulder, playfully, like guys do. It doesn't hurt, but I feel like crying anyway. Maybe you can figure out why. Maybe I have more depth than I'm letting on.

After they are gone, Lorraine asks me all sorts of questions.

Do you like to drink?

Yes.

What do you drink?

Pinot Noirs, mostly. But I won't say no to a good Cab.

It's got to be a real monster, though. There's nothing worse than a bad Cab.

Do you drink all the time?

Only when I'm conscious.

Are you in pain?

Only when I breathe.

She takes my blood pressure. The cuff feels tight, but Lorraine keeps pumping the little black bulb, making it even tighter. The sound the pump makes is like a woman on the verge of an orgasm, or what I *think* a woman on the verge of an orgasm sounds like, because I personally have never heard that sound. I've seen it, though, in porn movies, but I've got a feeling that some of those girls are faking.

Afterward, some big Black Guy in White comes by and shows me to my room. I am tired, but he tells me I have to take a shower, and I don't want to break The Rules. As I strip, I can hear Gloria Gaynor in my head, singing "I Will Survive." I *love* that song.

The water is hot. Burning hot. It scalds my skin. I guess I could simply reach over and adjust the temperature by, say, adding a little cold water to the mix, but that wouldn't make for good drama. So I take my punishment like a man. Like. A. Man.

The combination lock is still dangling from my left earlobe, and it hurts like a motherfucker. I wonder whether Lorraine noticed it, and, if she didn't, whether she's a good psychologist or psychiatrist or whatever. Then again, maybe she noticed it and didn't want to say anything. Maybe she is both maternal and tactful. That is a good combination. That makes me think of the combination lock again, and in some ways I am thankful. I realize that whoever plunged that thing through my lobe could have done worse. Much worse. I've heard stories. I've lived stories. I've made stories up.

When I get out of the shower, I think I see a shadow, but I'm not sure. Then I think I see bugs crawling up the wall, and I think the walls are breathing, expanding and contracting, closing in on me, but that's too *Lost Weekend*, so I ignore it.

I cross to the mirror, with a towel hanging loosely at my waist, like a hula skirt. The mirror is fogged up and I am glad because I don't want to see my face. I don't want to look into my own eyes for the simple yet heart-tugging reason that I haven't had the courage to look into my own eyes in many years. I do not want to see The Real Me. The Real Me is a coward. And a liar. But I have my good points, too. My prose, for example. And the way I use "and" repeatedly in very long sentences to create the illusion of breathlessness.

Aaargh! Here come the bugs! I am lost. Here come the Black Men in White, with their Big Fucking Syringes. Afterward, I wake up and hurl and find my way to The Lounge. I guess I'm early, because I'm alone, and I take a few moments to review my Life of Privilege. (Caps mine.)

Who am I?

What happened to my hopes and dreams?

When did everything begin to go wrong?

Wait. I am all over the place. Let's focus: Are there three or four key elements in my young, privileged life that shaped me and defined me, and do any of them have the Weight of Tragedy?

Before I can begin to answer these rudimentary questions, men start wandering in. They notice me, or half-notice me, until one of them *totally* notices me.

Hey, Dick Wad. That's my chair.

I don't understand him. Is he talking to me? Is that allowed? We're not remotely from the same socio-economic background. I mean, seriously, has this man ever even *heard* of seared foie gras?

DID YOU FUCKING HEAR ME, DICK WAD? THAT'S MY GODDAMN CHAIR!

I can feel The Fury thumping at my chest, from the inside, and I know I could beat this asshole to a Bloody Pulp, but that feels wrong, structurally and thematically, if not morally, so I decide to let him live.

Okay, I say. I will be happy to move.

Several guys stare at me, hostile, dismissive, and I know what they're thinking. They're thinking I'm a wuss. But they don't know me like I don't know me and don't want to know me. And, most of all, they don't know The Fury. If they ever get to know The Fury, watch out.

I look away, my head tilted at a haughty angle, dismissing them right back, and I study The Lounge with earnest superciliousness. I see a soda machine, a candy machine, and a coffee maker. Well slap my ass and call me Sally! I don't give a shit about the soda machine, the candy machine, or the coffee maker. I am thinking about Pinot Noir. And dancing. Always the dancing. I drink Pinot Noir. I Dance. I am Garbage.

What's that on your ear?

I turn around. Some guy with a butt like a sledgehammer is standing next to me, his mouth hanging open like he's not too bright. The effort of putting a sentence together seems to have has left him completely winded.

A combination lock, I say.

I can see that, he says. What happened to your eyes?

What do you mean?

You look like a fucking raccoon, pal.

I guess somebody hit me.

Did you hit him back?

He's in a fucking coma, motherfucker! You got any more stupid questions?

I don't know why I'm so aggressive. No, that's not true. I *do* know why. It's because there's a little too much homoeroticism in my writing, and I need to counterbalance it with healthy dollops of swaggering machismo. I do not think this is a bad thing. It worked for Hemingway. Why won't it work for me? I mean, if you take the notion of *talent* out of the equation.

You ever have anal sex? he asks me.

Excuse me?

He proceeds to tell me his sad story, which defies plausibility. Then again, all the stories that come out of this place are apocryphal and clichéd. My father raped me. My mother sold me for drugs. My dog died when I was seven and I haven't had sex since. (Think about *that* for a moment. Or don't.)

Suddenly, a Black Guy in a White announces that it's time for lunch, and everyone files out like they're in high school or something. When the room has emptied out, the Black Guy looks at me with such tenderness that I almost burst into tears.

Jimmy, he says gently. It's time for lunch.

I'm not hungry I say.

You don't have to eat, he says. But you have to Follow the Rules. Didn't Lorraine talk to you, *ad nauseum*, about the rules?

I find my way to the Mess Hall and get in line, and I know everyone is staring at me. I feel a little like Lindsay Lohan, in *Mean Girls*. I'm new here, and I'm desperate to be accepted, but I don't want them to know that.

I see a table across the room. There are some very Tough Looking Characters at the table, probably the toughest bastards in the place, and I know that that's where I belong. The question is, How do I make *them* know it?

Now I notice that the whole room feels as if it's tilted to one side, and I think I'm going to black out, so I Assume the Position, knees bent, arms out at my sides, ready to break the fall. But it's only the combination lock, weighing down my head. I tilt my head the other way and everything looks okay again. I think to myself, *If life were only that easy*. But for once I have the wherewithal not to say it out loud.

The line keeps moving but I see nothing that looks even remotely appetizing. Also, to be completely honest, I'm a little surprised that it's cafeteria-style, especially at these prices. I pass on the lasagna, the chicken cutlets, and the fish sticks, none of which look even remotely appetizing, and just as I'm beginning to run out of options I see that there's soup up ahead. Isn't that just like life? Right when you're on the verge of Abandoning All Hope, a Kindly Soul is waiting with Hot Soup. Well, not really.

When I get to the soup, I look at the woman who's ladling it out, and I am *totally shocked*. She looks exactly like Consuelo, our indentured servant, and in fact I am *sure* she must be Consuelo's twin sister.

Hijo de puta! I say (and this is an expression I picked up from Consuelo). *Tu tienes una hermana en Nueva York?*
She looks at me like I'm crazy.

What did you say? she asks me in flawless English.
I asked if you had a sister in New York, I say. Consuelo. From El Salvador.

No, I don't have a sister in New York, she says a bit testily. And I'm from the Philippines.

That really throws me. I've always wondered why

Hispanics and Filipinos are so hard to tell apart. And have you ever noticed the way Filipinos have really weird names that sound almost Hispanic? I mean, what is *that* about? Will someone please explain it to me? (Note to Fact Checking Department: If nothing else, please make sure I have spelled "Philippines" and "Filipino" correctly.)

Do you want soup or don't you?

Which soup would you recommend?

I'd recommend the minestrone, since that's the only soup we've got, but tomorrow I might recommend the bouillabaisse.

There's going to be bouillabaisse tomorrow? I ask, and for the first time since my arrival I feel a touch of optimism.

Okay, pal. Stop fucking around.

I'll take a bowl of the minestrone please.

She ladles it out and I thank her and move off, hoping The Fury doesn't get the better of me. Why did she have to lie to me about the bouillabaisse? Is that how she gets her kicks? Why is the world so full of twisted people?

I begin to look for an empty table, with the combination lock swinging from my lobe, keeping time, clicking along, and once again I get the sense that the whole place is staring at me. That might just be the Narcissistic Personality Disorder, however, though frankly I don't know why they call it a *disorder*. I've read the DSM-III, and I have studied the criteria. *An inflated valuation of self?* Check. *Expects preferential treat-ment without undertaking mutual commitments?* Check? *Displays supercilious imperturbability?* Check.

And the problem is . . . ?

I find a table and have a seat. I am alone, thankfully alone, as alone as the day I burst forth from my mother's womb, covered in filth and slime.

I begin ladling the hot soup into my mouth, and it burns. I guess I could wait for it to cool down, or maybe I could blow on it a little, like people do, but where's the drama in that?

I finish the soup, despite the searing hot pain, and I re-alize I am still hungry. I am *starving*, in fact. But it has nothing to do with regular hunger. This hunger is all about Filling That Big Hole Within. I am here be-cause I am Empty Inside.

I

Am

Empty

Inside

The Big Questions barrel toward me in a Proustian rush. Why am I alive? What does it all mean? Will somebody please take a moment to explain why the GPS system in my dad's car sometimes looks like it's upside down?

After lunch, as I am making my way back to The Lounge, avoiding eye-contact with the plebes, a guy approaches me in the corridor. He is dressed all in black, like a Ninja Warrior, and I think he looks ridiculous.

Jimmy, he says. My name is Chuck. I'm your Unit Recovery Counselor. I need to ask you a few questions. In the interesting of padding, I will walk you through them one at a time.

How'd you get that lock on your ear?

I don't know.

Have you tried getting it off?

I don't have the combination.

Does it hurt?

Yes.

I will see about having it surgically removed, but it's going to be the Most Painful Experience of Your Life.

Why?

Because you can't have any drugs during the procedure, not even Novocaine.

Novocaine? What does Novocaine have to do with anything? Isn't that for your teeth?

It doesn't matter. Whatever they use is just not going to happen. You are at Sleepy Hollow, and we have rules here.

Ad nauseum, I say.

Chuck then asks me when I started drinking, and I tell him it all began when I was seven, after I ran over that kid at the Bumper Car concession. (Well, not me, exactly, it was some guy in a *red* Bumper Car, earlier that morning, but *hearing* about it really affected me.) He asks me if I have ever blacked out, and I tell him I black out all the fucking time. He asks me when was the last time I blacked out, and I say I can't remember, but that a short time ago, in the cafeteria, I felt like I was *about* to black out. Then he asks me if I've ever thought about suicide, and I tell him I have—that I've thought about it every hour of every day for the past three years.

This isn't entirely true. I *haven't* thought about it. Or maybe I thought about it once or twice, in passing, which is the pretty much the way I think about everything. And if you *do* think about it, isn't suicide really kind of stupid? I mean, you know, if you're going to kill yourself, you have to do it on a day when you're *happy*. Everything is going great, the sun is shining, and this time you actually remembered the sunscreen. If on that perfect day you still feel like killing yourself, then by all means go ahead! But just about any idiot feels like killing himself when he's depressed. So it doesn't really make it special. Or smart. I don't share any of this with him, because I don't want him to think I've got logorrhea or anything, but suddenly I feel as if I'm in the grip of Tourette's and I jump to my feet, my fist clenched, and shout, ATTIKA!

Chuck recoils as if he's been slapped in the face.

Slapped

In

The

Face

I quickly sit down and act as if nothing has happened, hoping he might think he imagined the whole, bizarre incident. But no such luck.

What was that all about? he asks me.

Clearly Chuck has been living in a cave for the past decade or two. *Attika* is the second most popular daytime television Talk Show in broadcast history, and my parents have promised to TiVo every episode during my stay at Sleepy Hollow. To me, Attika, the *person*, is what America is all about. When you think that a young girl from Brownsville, Texas, the daughter of a ranch hand and an illegal immigrant, can rise to such prominence and power, and can become the Final Arbiter of Literary Taste in America, well—it brings the blood rushing to the back of my throat.

It's nothing, I say, and I gesture theatrically, as if I could sweep the very thought out of the room (and out of his mind).

It works. Chuck lets it slide. This is a good thing, because I don't want him to know that I have Literary Aspirations. Not long ago I reached a point where I realized I wasn't very good at anything, so I decided to become a writer. I haven't written anything yet, per se, but on those rare occasions when I actually think about committing something to paper I always ask myself, *What would Attika think?* This is my own personal version of *What would Jesus do?,* although I don't think much of Jesus, and I believe that that whole crucifixion thing was no more than a weird, sadomasochistic glorification of suffering—which I'm not into. (Okay, *once,* but I was out of my fucking mind on an amazing Australian Pinot, a Bass Phillip, 2001.) Still, I think every one of us feels like we have stories to tell—certainly every cab driver in New York does, or *did,* back when a few of them still spoke English— and I'm no exception. So I think about the future. And in my wildest dreams I sometimes see myself sitting on that red couch with Attika, propped against the very cushions that have cooed at so many famous buttocks.

Have you ever been arrested?

I snap out of my reverie. It's Chuck, still putting me through my paces. I want to lie to him, but I fight the urge. I *have* been arrested—once for jaywalking and once for urinating in public—but this is not what I tell him. I tell him that I've been arrested plenty— eleven times before I reached the age of twenty—and that my most recent arrest was for felony mayhem. After I say this, I wonder what felony mayhem means, if anything, and why I would say something like that, and I am frankly stymied. Chuck wants details, so I make up some cock-and-bull story about getting into a fist fight with a police officer, and I get a little carried away. Before I know it, shots are exchanged, a patrol car explodes, and I take a bullet though the cheek.

Well, he says. You are lucky to be alive, Jimmy.

You could say that, I say. Then again, you could not.

Do you want your old life back?

He stares at me, hard. I know he wants me to avert my eyes, but I refuse.

He asks me again, enunciating each world clearly: Do. You. Want. Your. Old. Life Back. Jimmy.

I guess so, I say, but I am thinking that my Old Life wasn't all that fucking good, so why would I want it back?

That's not going to cut it, he says. You have to really want it, Jimmy. Every person at Sleepy Hollow really wants it. That's the way it has to be, and even then— wanting it with all your heart and soul—is seldom enough.

How many people get their lives back? I ask.

Not many.

Give me a number.

Maybe fifteen percent.

That's terrible.

Not for the fifteen percent who make it.

What happens to the other eighty-five percent?

They come back. And they keep us in business.

So recidivism is good for the recovery racket?

I guess you could look at it that way, he says. It doesn't make us bad people, though.

I take a moment, then I say, I have to be honest with you, Chuck. I am not sure I believe this bullshit.

What bullshit?

I don't think I'm sick, Chuck. I don't think any of the Men and Women at this facility are sick.

Oh?

Having cancer or something is being sick. Having Parkinson's is being sick. Having Alzheimer's is being sick and *not even knowing it*. But what we have isn't being sick. We call it an illness to make excuses for ourselves, but it's not an illness, Chuck. It's a choice. IT'S A CHOICE!

Lower your voice, he says. I'm less than five feet away.

I'm sorry. I didn't realize I was shouting. I tend to get emotional about certain things, and this is one of them.

I can see that, he says.

It's what I believe. Not illness; choice. *It's a fucking decision. Each and every time.*

You know, Jimmy, it seems to me that you don't have much empathy for people like yourself.

I don't. I hate weakness. Especially in others.

Okay. That's enough for today. Do you want me to introduce you to some of the guys?

No. What do I have in common with those guys? I have hardly anything in common with myself.

Okay. That's cool.

Can I go back to my room?

After the lecture.

What lecture?

There are lectures here every day. They are mandatory. Keep your eye on the Events Board. They are always changing the times on us.

He stands up and I stand up and we shake hands and it is good.

One more thing, he says. You're on restroom duty starting tomorrow.

Restroom duty?

I know you miss your Pratesi sheets, Jimmy, but you're at Sleepy Hollow now. All of us have jobs here. Your job is to clean the Group Toilets.

Okay, I say.

And watch out for Mort.

Mort?

Mort will be making sure you keep the restroom clean. The guy is fucking nuts, but I seem to be the only one in this place who thinks so.

That was really reassuring. Thank you for sharing that.

Mort's got an amazing story, though. He was found floating down the Yellowstone River.

Floating down the Yellowstone? What do you mean?

Exactly what it sounds like. A transgender fly fisherman was out early one morning, getting ready to start his day, or *her* day, I can't remember which, and Mort went whipping by in a reed basket.

Wow! Just like Romulus and Remus!

Not quite. He was nineteen years old and drunk out of his fucking mind and singing at the top of his voice, but otherwise—yes. Just like them.

That's an amazing story.

It is, he says. But it's *nothing* compared to some of the Other Stories you're going to hear.

I'm not sure what he means by this, but I don't think

about it too deeply—as is my wont. I go to the lecture. There's a rumor that the speaker is going to be A Boy Named It, and the men are excited. Then we hear that this is not the case, that the Girl Who Had Mind-Blowing Sex With Her Father is going to be providing the day's entertainment. Then it changes again: it's that skinny, hot-looking Prozac Girl, with whom I'd consider having sex—if she asked me nicely.

The rumors just keep coming: It's the Guy Who Runs With Scissors. It's that Scandinavian Dude who tried to pass himself off as a poor, abused Navajo Indian boy. No, it's the Androgynous Creature with Big Hair and Big Glasses—the H.I.V.-positive, ex-prostitute, former drug addict. Or not.

All of these are merely rumors, or course, and all of them turn out to be false. Some dumpy middle-aged guy shows up and introduces himself as Bob Levesh, which I think is a mistake, since last names are verboten, and he begins to talk about the relationship between a sound mind and a healthy body, or vice versa. It doesn't make sense to me either way. Then he's talking about his father, who got run over by a garbage truck, and his mother, who in her grief threw herself in front of a subway train, and his sister, who turned to prostitution to support him and his younger brother, and who must have been pretty good in the sack because they ended up in a big, sprawling house in Po-quott, Long Island.

While he drones on, I see a guy across the room who

looks like Bill Pullman, the actor. I've never liked Bill
Pullman in anything. He strikes me as one of those
guys who spends a lot of time weighing his choices in
life, and always makes exactly the wrong choice. I'm
not saying the unexamined life is a good thing, because I hear it isn't, but the *over-examined* life seems
like it can be a real goddamn waste of time.

After the lecture, the men file out, and the guy who
looks like Bill Pullman comes over to me.

Hey you, he says.

Me?

Yeah. You with the fucking combination lock in
your ear.

What? I say.

Why do you keep calling me Bill Pullman?

I never called you Bill Pullman. I've never seen you
before in my life. We've never had a conversation.

But you think I *look* like Bill Pullman?

Maybe a little. You have the same tortured eyes. Or
maybe you just need glasses.

Another man comes up, a guy I recognize as being
part of the Tough Bastard clique, even though he
looks like a Jewish accountant, and he tells Bill to take
a walk. He puts a friendly hand on my shoulder and
leads me away.

You called him Bill, I say, confused. That's not really
Bill Pullman, is it?

Of course not. That's Ralph M. He used to be the
Captain of a Fishing Boat in Nantucket, happily mar-

ried, father of three, and he threw it all away to become a gigolo.

A gigolo? That's weird. The guy must be fifty years
old, and, frankly, he's not that good-looking.

Well, you're right, Jimmy. It would have been nice if he
had had a friend like you, to help him face the truth,
but most of us are incapable of handling the truth.

What happened to him?

What happens to fifty-year-old men who launch new
careers as gigolos and fail?

I don't know, I say. They end up at Sleepy Hollow?

Benny nods, clearly impressed with my acumen.

I could tell you were smart, he says. The Other Guys
don't think you're that smart, but we'll show them.

Not smart? I protest. They don't even know me.

They're not bad guys, Jimmy. Except for maybe Alan
T. and Larry S.

How come everyone uses initials here? I feel like I'm
in a Kafka story.

"I wonder if I should marry F.? Or perhaps I should
wait until she tells me the rest of the letters in her
name."

Is that Kafka?

No, I think it's Woody Allen doing Kafka. And, if it's
not, it should be.

Who are you?

My name is Benny. Benny M. I used to work for the
government, taking care of people who didn't always
share the interests of this Great Country of ours.

Are you serious?

You don't think this is a Great Country?

I never said that. I was talking about that oblique reference to Covert Ops.

Jimmy, you seem to be stuck in some kind of Adolescent Fantasy, but go ahead and believe what you want to believe.

Are you saying you weren't in Covert Ops?

I was a *waiter*, Jimmy. At the White House dining room.

I shake my head. I can't believe the *characters* in this place!

Benny puts his arm around my shoulder and begins to lead me away.

There's something I want you to know, Jimmy. It may not seem relevant now, but someday, weeks from now, maybe even years from now, you'll remember this story.

What story?

I have a close friend who wrote a book, not a particularly compelling book, mind you—I think the most intellectually interesting thing about it was his unusual use of capital letters. I am still trying to figure out why "Grocery Store" is capitalized, but "bird" isn't.

Maybe he had a bad experience with a bird, I say, trying to be helpful. My brother's Insane First Wife was terrified of birds. That's what she said in court, anyway.

Maybe. But let's get back to the point. The point is that his book was rejected by seventeen publishers.

Poor bastard. What did he do?

It's not what he did, Jimmy, it's what he's *doing*. He is still trying. And that's what I want you to do. When things look bad, when they look hopeless even, I want you to *just hold on*. Can you do that for me?

Just hold on?

I known, I know. It's actually really lame advice, because you wouldn't be here if you could just fucking hold on, but it's the best I can do.

I feel like crying. And when I see tears in Benny's eyes, my own tears come hard and fast and true. I think, Jesus Christ. This story isn't even half over and there's been so much crying I feel like I'm on *American Idol*.

What's that? Jimmy says. A tattoo.

He slides my Rolex down a little. There's a simple if ragged tattoo that I keep hidden under my watch. Four little letters, J-I-A-L.

JIAL? Benny says. What the hell's that supposed to mean?

It's supposed to spell Jail. J-A-I-L. My tattoo artist was dyslexic.

You did time?

Uh huh.

Benny looks at me like he doesn't believe me.

I don't want to get into it now, Benny. Maybe when I get to know you better.

That's fine, Jimmy.

Thanks for being so understanding.

Don't mention it. Now go off and take care of those toilets. And Jimmy: Try to do a good job.

I use Windex on the bowls and the mirrors, with paper towels, because it seems to work just fine. It comes out pretty good, and I don't find the work all that distasteful.

The rest of the day goes by in a *lidded daze*, but shortly after I fall asleep I have a terrible dream. I am twenty-three years old. I am at The Roxy, dancing. Everyone is laughing at me.

I wake up screaming, and a Black Guy in White shows up. He looks like every other Black Guy in White, but maybe that's just me.

You had what they call a Dancer Dream, he tells me after I describe what happened.

Are they common? I ask.

Everyone has them.

Will they stop?

In time, he says. You have to be patient.

He starts singing a soothing, Negro lullaby, and I think back to my childhood. Playing with the little nappy-haired Negro children on our big property in Savannah. Listening to the workers, who make the dense woods reverberate with their soulful songs. Going down to the river with my friend Rufus to see if the catfish is bitin'. As I drift off, I realize that this is someone else's childhood, and that I seem to have usurped another person's reality, and not a very compelling one at that.

I also realize that I have gone a full twenty-four hours without dancing. I am scared, but I am also a little proud of myself. I hope you are proud of me, too.

2.

In the morning, I wake up feeling somewhat refreshed. I think back to the first chapter and feel confident that I have successfully created a character people will be rooting for. And I have done this by asking myself the right questions: *What sets the story in motion?* (Dancing.) *What is the story about?* (Me and My Recovery.) *Why will anyone care?* (Because I'm lovable and mostly because I'm flawed and because people respond to flawed characters who Struggle to Change.) *Will the hero* (Me) *attain his goal?* (Stay tuned!)

I go to breakfast and Benny invites me to sit with the Tough Characters. I'm not very good with names, but I remember that one of them is an undercover cop, another one runs an escort service, a third is a Harvard professor who has spent seventeen years studying the effects of dietary fat on the body (hint: it doesn't make you fat), and the last one is a brilliant attorney who gave away all of his earthly possessions, went off to India to find himself, and returned two weeks later and tried to get his shit back.

After breakfast, I go to the Medical Unit to get my meds. The Male Nurse waits until I've taken them, then tells me to report to the Entrance to the Hospital, where John Q. will be waiting for me in a White Transportation Van.

I go outside and John Q. is indeed waiting next to a White Transportation Van. He is a big bear of a man, with a penchant for young girls, and he's not much in the looks department, but I get the feeling he is Some-one Who Will Become a Friend and Ally, and I know I will make use of him later, when I have to help push the plot along.

Come here, he says. You look like you could use a hug. I don't know how he knows this, but he's right. I long for the simple pleasure of human contact, but I've never known how to ask for it. John comes close and takes me in his arms and hugs me. Even though I know there is nothing wrong with this, especially in our post-*Brokeback* world, I am a little self-conscious, and John senses it. He lets me go, and I can breathe again, and he says, I love you, man!

He says it like John Belushi used to say it when he was alive. I make this distinction because I have seen John Belushi since his death, but that's another amazing story, and I am thinking of saving it for my next book.

Where are we going? I ask John.

John tells me that we are going into town to see "Doc"

about removing the combination lock, and he says it is going to Hurt Like a Motherfucker. He tells me words alone will not be able to describe the pain I am going to feel, because the pain I am going to feel is ineffable. I am not sure that he is using that word correctly, but I let it slide. A lot of people who subscribe to that New Word a Day thing on their computers get them wrong.

As we drive along, toward town, I try not to think about the pain, because I am happy that I am going to get this lock removed once and for all. Last night, the lock, along with the Dancer Dreams, kept me up. I wonder if the lock is some kind of symbol. My vices are keeping the real me Locked In, for example. Or maybe the little black round dial with the tiny, white, numberless dashes along the outer edge are the Hands of Time, which spin one way and another, directionless, unless you know the combination. If I had to choose one of those two interpretations, I would choose the latter.

When we get to town, I see that it isn't much of a town. It has one street, called, predictably enough, Main Street (though I think it should be called Only Street), with a grocery store, a hardware store, a coffee shop, a little shithole bar with a broken neon-sign in the window, and a barbershop. The doctor's office is above the barbershop, and this resonates for me somehow, as if it should have historical significance.

John takes me upstairs, along the rickety wooden

steps, our footfalls echoing in the small space in slow and manifold progression, and we run into a Woman and her Young Son, on their way out. They are in an awful hurry and look very upset. The boy is crying, and I think, *Dear God, please don't let him grow up to be like me.* I have no reason to think this, and I conclude that this is yet another manifestation of my Narcissistic Personality Disorder, but I decide that—like much else in life—it isn't worth overanalyzing.

When we step into the office, I can see why the Boy Like Me and his mother were so upset. The Doctor is totally wasted, which for some reason reminds me of Svetlana—the exchange student to whom I lost my virginity (though she later denied it).

John! he bellows. How the fuck are you?

Hello, Doc.

Who's this? he says, slurring his words and turning to look at me.

Then he sees the combination lock and starts laughing. I laugh, too, a short, quick, seal-like burst, because I am nervous, but he is laughing so hard that I can't even hear my own laughter. He is doubled over with laughter, and then he's coughing, and then he's laughing again, and then he's struggling to catch his breath. It takes a long time for the Doctor to pull himself together, and by this time I am a little worried, though not for him. He apologizes for his unseemly outburst, asks me if I don't see the humor in the situation, which I don't, and then decides it's time to get to

work. I do not think this is a good idea, and I take
John aside and tell him that I wouldn't let that doctor
take my goddamn temperature, especially with that
other type of thermometer, but John begs me to let the
man do his job.

He is one of our success stories, he tells me.

Excuse me?

At Sleepy Hollow.

That's a Sleepy Hollow success story?

Come on, man, John says. Have a fucking heart.

I decide to let the Doctor take a look. For the first few
minutes, he decides he can "guess" the combination,
and he tries several times, always ending with that
trademark *yank* (to see if he finally got it right), and it
hurts like a motherfucker every time. Finally, he goes to
the window and hollers, Hank! I need you right now!

A few moments later, we hear footfalls on the stairs,
and a very thin, very old man walks inside in a
monkey-suit. His name, Hank, is stitched across the
top in cursive, but it looks like he sewed the letters on
himself. They are all over the place. Sort of like this,
H a n *k*, but not exactly.

Hank doesn't laugh when he sees the lock hanging
from my ear. Instead, he turns pale, and his hands begin to shake a little.

I know you can do this, Hank, the Doctor says.

I—I can't, Doc.

Hank begins to back away, but the Doctor grabs him
by the lapels and puts his face right up against his, and

shouts, Yes, you can, Hank! I AM TELLING YOU YOU CAN!

I turn to look at John, even as my testicles shrivel up, and I ask him, Is Hank a graduate of Sleepy Hollow, too?

John nods. I am sure that Hank has an Amazing Story of his own, maybe going back to his days as a fighter pilot with the Lafayette Escadrille, in World War I, and his liaison with that French farm girl who became his first wife, and who later caught him having congress with a cow, but I don't want to hear it. I've heard so many Amazing Stories that I hunger for Normalcy.

For the next three minutes—the length of time it takes the average American male to reach an orgasm, including foreplay—the Doctor and Hank argue about how to tackle my little problem, which is going to hurt like a motherfucker.

I finally get so sick of listening to this endless back and forth that The Fury makes a brief appearance.

I get it! I shout. No meds! No pain-killers. It's going to hurt. But so fucking what? I've been through a lot worse.

I see a pencil on the table and I pick it up.

Don't worry about me, I say. I'll just bite on this.

Well, as it turns out, I am wrong. I have never been through anything close to that kind of pain in my entire, tortured life. It is Beyond Worse. It is the Worst Pain I have ever experienced, times seven, squared. I would have rather been poked in the eye with a sharp stick.

In a rare moment of lucidity, I wonder why Hank and

the Doctor are singing Top Forty hits at the tops of their voices, then I realize it is simply to drown out my girlish screams.

I bite through the pencil. I eat it. I realize it's a chocolate pencil, and I decide it probably belonged to the little boy I saw leaving the office, the one who Mustn't Grow Up to Be Like Me, and all I can think is, *I hope there aren't any cooties on it.*

The pain just keeps coming, washing over me in terrible, electrifying waves. Every hair on my head stands up. Every muscle flexes. Every testicle I own shudders.

How are you holding up? the Doctor asks me.

Do what you need to do, I say. *Just get it over with.*

I cannot believe how fucking tough I am, nor how strong and steady beats my heart, but there you have it. Then I am begging for mercy, trying to get up, but Hank bitch-slaps me, hard, looking like he's enjoying it, and removes his belt. I think he is about to go all *Deliverance* on me, but he simply uses the belt to strap me down. I pass out.

Suddenly I see myself running through a field of flowers in the Swiss Alps, near St. Moritz, with Heidi R., the first girl I ever loved. This is not a dream. This really happened to me. I was at an Elite Boys Boarding School, near town, and Heidi was in a nearby Finishing School, somewhat less elite, but still quite expensive. She had beautiful golden braids, and, to this day, whenever I see the braided ropes on, say, a hammock, I get an erection.

I loved Heidi more than Life Itself. One day we went skiing, as a group, but Heidi and I managed to get a lift to ourselves, and we decided to meet at the edge of a run called *Le Con du Diable*. I think that's French for *The Devil's Ass*, but I'm not sure. There were some pay toilets nearby, and I checked to make sure I had the correct change, and we both knew that this was the day we were going to lose our virginity together.

Just before the lift reached the top, Heidi fondled my penis, but it was hard to feel much through my thick ski pants and long underwear. Still, the promise of the gesture remained with me for many years afterward.

Twenty minutes later, I was waiting for Heidi at the edge of *The Devil's Ass*, when I saw her barreling toward me. She was smiling, grinning with sweaty lust, her golden braids flying behind her in the crisp, mountain air, but just then one of her skis caught an edge and she lost her balance. As I watched in mute horror, she flew right past me and went over the side.

I never told anyone about this. That's just one of *two* horrible stories I have kept inside me my whole life, festering like a sebaceous cyst. The other one involves an Evil Mime. But I'm getting ahead of myself here.

When I regain consciousness, I am still in the chair. The Doctor and Hank and John B. are right in my face, and they look distorted, as if I'm seeing them through one of those little fish-eye lens door thingies. How you doing, pal?

I don't know who says this. The words are distant and

inaccessible, and seem to echo off the walls, growing fainter and more distant with each passing second, as echoes do. How you doing, pal? How you doing, pal? How you doing, pal?

My heads lolls, and I see that the floor to my left is pooled with blood. The Doctor is standing in the blood, and for the first time I notice that he is wearing Z-Coils. They are these weird, boingy-looking shoes with big, industrial-style springs in the heels, and they're supposed to free you from back pain forever. I wish I could describe them better, but I'm not that good a writer. I think they have a website, though, with pictures—if you're interested.

Jimmy? Can you hear me?

It's John, my Friend and Ally. John the Hugger.

I nod, but I hardly have the energy for that.

This man needs medical attention, the Doctor tells John.

I find this odd, and it doesn't wholly compute. Isn't he a doctor? And if he isn't a doctor, what is he? And why is he allowed to operate as if he *were* a doctor?

If anything happens to this man, I will not be held accountable, the Doctor says.

I wanted to be a doctor once, because my Whole Life has been geared toward helping people. But instead of going to medical school, I took the money and went to Oregon's Willamette Valley and spent a few months sampling their various Pinot Noirs. Some of them were ripe, and well-balanced, and had nice, chewy tannins. Others were a little hot, and burned on their way down, and others still had a good, long finish, though it wasn't always a *pleasant* finish, and sometimes I had to kill it with a strong, dark beer. Some of the Pinots were as fat and flabby as Maria, who predated Consuelo, and who had been stealing from my parents for the better part of three years, but who was always willing to throw a leg over whenever I stumbled into the maid's quarters.

Jimmy? Jimmy, you're babbling.

Oh, I say. Did I say that out loud?

Yes.

I was just kidding about Maria. Nothing ever happened between us.

This man needs medical attention, the Doctor repeats, ignoring me. He has lost a lot of blood.

I signal to John, who comes close and helps me to my feet.

I am in excruciating pain. Everything is white. *There is white. Everywhere there is white.* I can hardly breathe. Hardly at all. Breathe. Did I mention that I am still in tremendous pain? Indescribably hot, searing, white, stab-me-with-a-bayonet pain, pain beyond anything a mere mortal would be able to endure (me excluded). I also suspect that there's not much left of my ear, but I don't care. I turn to look at the doctor, and I stare right into his eyes, as baleful as a puppy, with the kind of intensity that would make Martin Buber blush, and I say, Thank you, doctor.

For what? He asks.

Well, you know, if I had even a soupçon of doubt about the existence of God prior to this marvelous experience, which I didn't, I now know that he couldn't possibly exist, because I've done a lot of bad things in my life, including pleasuring myself in a pay toilet in the Swiss Alps while Heidi lay at the bottom of a ravine in a crumpled heap, dying, with one of her own ski poles protruding from her neck, but I've never done anything bad enough to justify this kind of pain.

You sure you're okay, pal? John asks me.

Yes, I say. Never better!

Maybe I should take you to the hospital, like Doc says.

No no! I'm telling you! I feel fucking great!

Then I pass out.

I pass out.

I

Pass

The

Fuck

Out

3.

When I wake up, back at Sleepy Hollow, in my own bed, I feel marginally better. I get up, brush my teeth without looking at my reflection in the mirror, and go off to get breakfast, which is also self-serve. As I'm standing in line, I see a girl that looks a little like Angelina Jolie, but squat, with thin Crack Ho lips, and with dark bags under her dull, brown eyes. In short, she has nothing at all to recommend her, but I sense something there—a Great Sadness that she wears like an ill-fitting frock—and I have always been drawn to sadness, especially if it holds the promise of Easy Sex. Alas, we are not allowed to talk to the women here, and they are not allowed to talk to us, so there is nothing I can do to assuage her pain. In a moment, she will go off to the Women's Side of the cafeteria, and I will be left with nothing, not even hope.

As I am thinking about the futility of my situation, Angelina drops her fork. She bends over to pick it up and I see that her culottes are ripped and a tad unclean. This excites me for some reason, a reason I prefer not to analyze too deeply, and I make an effort to think about something else. I think of that terrible accident I may have caused on the Little League field, almost two decades ago now, and I feel bad for that poor, dorky kid, Dave F. Then again, I hear it turned out all right. I hear his parents decided to raise him as a girl, at the suggestion of the doctors, and that the result was nothing short of astonishing. My mother ran into his family once, at dinner, at Le Cirque, (a place they would never have been able to afford were it not for that incredibly generous settlement), and she told me that Dave had turned into a lovely young woman. Suddenly I'm really weirded out. What if I meet a girl in a bar some day, and I take her home, and she turns out to be Dave F.? What would we talk about? The Old Days on Little League? At least we'd have *that* in common, I guess. That makes me think about some of the dogs I've gone home with right around Last Call—real double-baggers. You know the expression, right? You wear a bag over your head, and you put a bag over *her* head just in case your bag falls off. That, in turn, gets me thinking of that old country-western tune, the one about how all the girls start looking pretty good right around closin' time, but before I can remember the lyrics I have arrived at the Cool Table. As I sit down, I see that Elliot is holding court.

Why did I go into the escort business? Because people are lonely, and I knew I could capitalize on that. We are all looking for love, guys. We *need* love. Without a woman at our side, even it's only for an hour, we are nothing.

A lively discussion follows. It covers loneliness, the nature of love, and our all-too-human desire to connect, and while I get the distinct impression that none of it is original, I still find it oddly compelling:

Benny: Loneliness is absolute. To expect otherwise is an illusion.

Danny: All this talk about "happiness" is nonsense. My greatest happiness consists in getting a good blow-job.

Larry: The black hole of self-absorption is bottomless. We only give a shit about ourselves.

Alan: Our romantic expectations are unsustainable.

Michael: I should never have given away the couch from Roche Bobois. That's what I miss most.

Alan: The honeymoon always ends. Romance is unsustainable.

Larry: Love is an endless cycle of impossible expectations followed by bitter disappointments.

Michael: And how the prices have soared! My God, I can't even afford *one* of their leather chairs now, let alone an entire couch.

Alan: There is no escape from human solitude.

Danny: The shelf life of passion is six months, tops.

Benny: If you expect another person to make you happy, you are fucking meshuga.

These guys not only have amazing stories, but all of

them are Erudite Beyond Belief (except maybe Michael, who might be a tad more brilliant than the others, but who tends to be one-dimensional and obsessive, especially about material goods). Suddenly I begin to think about the types of people that end up in places like Sleepy Hollow, and it strikes me that it's always the Best Type of People—people who are too sensitive for the world; people who feel too deeply. I am in no way suggesting that *I* am one of those people, and I don't for a moment think I belong in their company, or that I deserve to breathe the same rarefied air they breathe, but don't let me sway you. Think what you want to think.

As I leave the table, I can't stop reviewing all of the brilliant and near-brilliant things they said, and I can barely make the center hold. Like most completely self-absorbed people, I only think of the world as it relates to me, and everything they said relates to me. I *am* lonely! I want desperately to be in love! I want to be able to look into a woman's eyes and know that she's the one, that she's my Magical Missing Half, but where am I going to find such a woman?

Jimmy!

I look up. It's Lorraine. She's standing at the door to her office, looking at me in that maternal way she has, but with one of her hips cocked a little, like a streetwalker, so once again I am confused.

Come here, Big Guy.

You talkin' to me? I say.

It's time for your MMPI.

My what?

Didn't I tell you about it? I thought I told you. You have to take a test.

I don't feel like it, I say. I'm in the grip of an idea that's Larger Than Me, Larger Than Both of Us, Really, an idea that speaks to the commonality of human experience. *If you prick us, do we not bleed?*

Put it on the back burner for now, she says. This is a very important test. The sooner you take it, the sooner we'll be able to determine how best to help you, and that's why you're here, Jimmy. To get better.

I feel like walking away, but one of those Black Guys in White is standing at the end of the corridor, with his big black arms folded across his chest, studying me. He looks like that big black guy in *The Green Mile*. They *all* do, come to think of it, but maybe that's part of my pathology. I remember going out to Los Angeles some years ago, when I thought I might want to get into the movie business, and all of the women looked exactly alike to me. It was freaky. I thought I had this whole Oliver Sacks thing going on: *The Man Who Couldn't Tell One Woman in Los Angeles from Every Other Woman in Los Angeles.* And it went beyond the women. I would go to these people's houses, and even these were indistinguishable. I guess they all hired the Same Designer. They all had the same Kertesz prints, probably unsigned, and the big round dining table with the eight mismatched, one-of-a-kind chairs, and koi. The fucking koi were everywhere, like aquatic rats.

Jimmy?

I look up at Lorraine.

Come on, she says. Let's get it over with.

I follow her into the room. The room is white. Everything is white. But it's a *different* white than last time. I wonder if she redecorated since I was last here, or whether I'm disoriented and I'm in another room entirely.

How's the ear look?

I don't know. I haven't seen it yet. I won't see it till the bandages come off.

I hear you were very courageous.

I was, I say.

It's not like I'm trying to show off or anything, but I need to communicate, early in the narrative, that I'm the kind of guy who can do anything I set my mind to. Because here's the thing you need to know about drama: you don't want to bore people by telling them *everything* about your protagonist. Instead, you create a scene that puts him (or her) in an Intensely Challenging Situation—i.e., having his ear butchered—and you discover Who He Is through his handling of that situation. Comprende?

Lorraine shows me to a table. There is a booklet there,

stapled together, and across the front I see the words *Minnesota Multiphasic Personality Inventory-2*.

What is this? I ask.

It's nothing to worry about. Think of it as a psychological profile. It's designed to help us identify your problems.

We know what my problems are. I drink Pinot Noir, I Dance, I am Garbage. Sometimes I feel like punching three holes in a trash bag, sticking my arms and head through them, and going out and showing the world who and what I really am.

I drink Pinot Noir.

I Dance.

I am Garbage.

We want to dig a little deeper, she says.

I don't want to dig deeper. I *think* this, but I don't *say* it. I prefer to swim on the surface of life, like those water-spiders up at Lac Notre Dame. I could sit there and watch them all day, if I've had enough to drink. And by the way, parenthetically speaking, I liked Pinot Noir long before *Sideways* came out. I knew everything there was to know about it. I knew it was a temperamental, risky grape, one that often came up short, just as I knew that—when it hit—a Pinot really was the Holy Grail of wines. I knew all about the younger blends, with their hint of violet and bougainvillea, and I was familiar with the way the wine became transformed as it aged, developing those rich, muddy, impish flavors to which I have become addicted.

Jimmy!

I'm sorry. I was thinking.

What were you thinking about?

Nothing. *Life.*

There's nothing to it, she says. Everything is either True or False.

It is?

On the *test*, Jimmy. The questions.

So I have a fifty-fifty chance of getting them right?

It's not about getting them right. It's about getting *you* right.

I don't want to disappoint you, I say.

You won't disappoint me. You could never disappoint me.

That was heavy. I wonder why she would say something like that. She doesn't even know me.

Then, with gravitas, she adds, The only person you have to worry about disappointing is yourself.

Man, I can see she really *does* like to dig deep. I have no answer for her. I'm sure I'll have one the moment she leaves the room. I'll think of something really witty to say, but she'll be gone. The French have an expression for that. It's called *esprit de l'escalier.* Roughly translated, it means *staircase wit.* You're on the stairwell, on your way home from a bad party, where someone has tried to humiliate you, fairly successfully, by calling you an irresponsible drunk and a pathological liar, and suddenly—when it's too late—you think of a witty riposte. "Your mother wears army boots!" Or something like that. But good.

There are two sharp pencils on the desk, Lorraine is saying. Try not to hurt yourself.

What do you mean?

That was a little stab at humor, Jimmy. I'm a brilliant psychiatrist, and I know my way around a penis, but that doesn't mean I don't have a sense of humor.

I'll keep that in mind, I say.

Good luck.

I didn't think I needed luck.

It's just an expression, Jimmy. That's not what I meant.

Then what did you mean?

Try to relax, okay? Everything you do seems drowned in mental considerations.

I don't understand you. One minute you tell me I don't think enough, the other you tell me I think too much.

She rolls her eyes and leaves the room and I turn my attention to the test.

Most of the questions are easy. Yes, I consider myself to be a stable person. No, I don't often think of death. Yes, the world is aligned against me. (On this particular question, I find myself adding, in very small letters, **Especially my parents**.)

After answering five hundred and sixty-seven questions, with the greatest of ease, I finally get to the Last
Question, and it really throws me.

The question is, *My sins are unpardonable.*

True or False?

My

Sins

Are

Unpardonable

True   or   False?

I think about Bumper Cars. I think about Little
League and the mysteries of human sexuality. I think
about Heidi, whom I will always associate with the
smell of fresh snow and pay toilets. Then I think
about jaywalking, and about urinating in public, and
about felony mayhem—and about taking a bullet in
the cheek. Have I sinned? Are these sins, or am I human, like you? Flawed, like you? Lost, like you? Are we
not Brothers and Sisters? Are we not basically The
Same? Are we not One People, trying to make sense
of this crazy business of living? And, most importantly,
When you look at me, do you not see yourself?

And what does this mean, *Unpardonable?*

From whom should I seek forgiveness?

It seems to me that if I have betrayed anyone, it is
myself.

I slam my fist against the table, making the pencils
jump, then I take a deep, bracing breath, get to my feet,
and leave the room.

I feel like calling my friends, but I don't have any friends, and I don't like the two that still talk to me.

I call my parents and my mother answers the phone.

Hi, Mom.

Jimmy! My God, son. It's so nice to hear from you. How are you?

I am deeply conflicted.

About what, son? Wait a minute. Harold! It's Jimmy. Pick up the line!

My father gets on the line. Hey champ, he says. I'm on the other line, on hold with my friend Janos, in Caracas, but I'll take a minute from my busy schedule to talk to you: How you doin', boy?

It's strange, whenever my father pretends he cares, his voice changes. He sounds like he's from Texas or something.

I don't know, I say. I'm trying to get a grip on this. I'm trying to understand why I'm here. Most of all I'm trying to understand why two wonderful people— two normal, stable, decent people like yourselves— were saddled with a son like me.

Son! Gotta ride! That's my little Hungarian buddy on the other line.

He hangs up.

Wow, I say. Do I even exist for you guys? Do you sometimes wish you never had me? I bet you do.

My mother begins to cry. No, she says.

The truth, Mom. *The truth is what matters. Remember the truth. It is all that matters.*

She takes a moment, sniffling a little. Yes, she says finally, but not often.

Yes what? I ask, because I've lost my train of thought.

Yes, we sometimes wish we never had you.

I knew it!

But we're not the only ones. On Saturday, we were out with the Dunns and the Schwartzes—you remember them, don't you, dear? Lovely people, *some of them,* anyway. And they were saying the same things.

What? That they wished you never had me?

No. They wished they had never had their own children.

After I get back to my room, I sit there for a moment, lost in deep, troubling thought, then I also hang up. I wonder who I am. I wonder why there are people like me in the world. I wonder why I must deliberately hurt those I love. And, more important, why they must hurt me.

I feel sick. *Everything that I know and that I am and everything that I've done begins flashing in front of my eyes.*

Jimmy!

It's one the Black Guys in White. Man, they are everywhere—and I mean that in the nicest possible, non-racist way.

What?

Mort wants to see you in the Group Toilets.

Why?

I don't know. But he's waiting for you, so I have a feeling you're going to find out.

Some people! You give them a little power, they get attitude.

I go to the restroom. Mort is sitting on the counter, his ass propped next to the sink, and he doesn't look exactly thrilled.

Hey, Mort. I say. You wanted to see me?

The fucking toilets are filthy.

Excuse me?

You heard me. FILTHY FILTHY FILTHY! I want them sparkling, or you're out. O-A-T, OUT.

It's O-U-T. U, not A. The way you said it, it spells "oat."

FUCK YOU, RICH BOY! You think you're better than me because you went to Harvard?

I didn't go to Harvard. My grades were lousy. I had to finish high school through one of those correspondence courses you read about on the covers of matchbooks. I ended up at Lake Forest College, near Chicago. It was okay, but I was not well-liked. I've been an Outcast my whole life.

You know something, Pinocchio? You're weird.

Who told you my last name? There aren't supposed to be last names.

Instead of answering, he cups his hand over his mouth and makes like he's Darth Vader. Jimmy, he says. I am your father. Prepare to die.

I get the impression that he's linking two unrelated movies together—*Star Wars* and *The Princess Bride*—and I try to set him straight.

I get the "Luke, I am your father" bit, I say. But the "prepare to die" bit is from another movie. Mandy Patinkin. Spanish accent. Remember? I do the accent for him. "Hello, my name is Iñigo Montoya. You killed my father. Prepare to die."

The fucking toilets are filthy, he repeats.

Maybe they are now, I say, and I glance over at them and see that they are indeed filthy. But when I cleaned them this morning, or yesterday morning, or maybe even the morning before—how the fuck long have I been here, anyway?—they were super-clean.

You're in big trouble, Jimmy P.

I am upset, but then I remember what Benny told me. *Just hold on.* What the fuck does that mean? I've been hanging on by my fingernails for most of my life, so what the fuck am I supposed to hold on *to*?

Mort gets off the counter, gives me a dirty look, and walks out. I can see he is going to be immensely difficult, which is okay. In stories like this, in any story, really, even in comedies, you are always looking for an Antagonist, and I believe I have found mine. Mort is the Villain in the piece, and I hark back to the old saw: *The bigger the villain, the better the story.* I have a feeling this is going to be a very good story indeed. Mort may not be Hannibal Lecter, especially in the Looks Department, but he is crazy as a loon, and as such represents a serious threat to my recovery—nay, to my Very Existence.

4.

The next morning, I get up super early and I clean the restroom really well. I find all sorts of cleaning supplies in a closet in the hallway, and I spend two hours on my hands and knees, scrubbing and shining and buffing. I want to impress Mort, partly because that's the kind of guy I am, and partly because he scares the shit out of me.

At the breakfast line, I find myself right behind Angelina. She keeps slowing down, and at one point she bumps my crotch with her elbow. I think this is an accident, but then she does it again, *twice*, and I get a little wood. I wonder if she's trying to tell me something.

I go to my regular table, and everyone is there except Benny, my mentor and friend. I start eating my oatmeal, which is grey and mushy, just like it's supposed to be, and I learn that Benny is in the infirmary.

I hope it isn't anything serious, I say. Like cancer. Or one of those real illnesses.

I don't say this last part out loud, because I don't know how the guys feel about my *Real Illness versus Choice* theory, and I wouldn't want to alienate them. You already know how I feel about it, so I don't have to repeat myself, but I will anyway: We are in this place because we are weak. And that goes for every last one of us. We are weak and we are losers and we are doing what we do by *choice*. Nobody pointed a gun at my head and said, "Dance, Jimbo, dance!" Well, now that I think of it, somebody did point a gun at my head, once, in the Viper Room, in L.A. Well, it wasn't *me* exactly. I was dancing with Paris and Nicole, or *near* them, anyway, back when they were still talking, before that whole ugly business with the video tape, and a guy that Paris had never slept with pulled a gun on her and said, "You're coming with me, you vacuous, empty-headed byatch!" I wrestled him to the ground, and a shot rang out, and no one was hit, but a bottle of the good Stoli exploded, and I had to pay for it. I think Paris should at least have offered to pay for it, but she didn't. And I'm not saying that that makes her a bad person, but it certainly colored my opinion.

After breakfast, I am told I have visitors. This strikes me as odd. I can only conclude that it must be my parents, since they're the only people who know I'm here. When I go out to the visitor's area, I discover I am mistaken. It's not my parents at all. It's my friend Howard A., and my other friend, Nigel M., though they're not really my friends. I owe them money.

Hey guys, I say, smiling falsely. How's it going?

Great, Howard says. Just came by to see how you were doing.

That is such bullshit! They are worried about their money!

It's good to see you guys. How did you find me?

Your mother told us you were here, Nigel says.

I don't believe this for a minute. I think they probably hired a Private Investigator.

What's that? I say. You brought me presents?

We did, yes. Howard says.

We tried to think of something appropriate, Nigel says.

I open my presents. Both of them are books. One of them is called *How to be Idiotically Happy*. I've never been much of a believer in this self-help business, but you never know. And it has a great review on the cover by Hunter S. Thompson: "This book changed my life!"

The other book is called, *Love Me Tender, Love Me Raw*. It looks interesting. Thematically, it's very much in line with what we were talking about recently at the Cool Table, and it drives home the point that—at the end of the day—people just want to be loved. I know I do. How about you? This one has a quote from Ernest Becker, who is identified as the author of *The Denial of Death*. "We are all hopelessly absorbed with ourselves. If we care about anyone, it is usually ourselves first." To me, that doesn't seem particularly apt for a book about love, but then—what do I know about marketing?

This is really nice of you guys, I say. I'm moved almost to tears.

You know, Nigel says. I'm the one who put you in the cab that night, with the towel-head.

Oh Jesus! Really? I was wondering about that. Was I totally fucked up?

That's an understatement.

What happened?

You don't want to know, Nigel says. But if you hear from a guy called Boris, it could get ugly.

Nigel is right: I don't want to know.

How long are you going to be here? Howard asks.

That's a good question, I say. I am free to walk out of here at any time, which is what makes it such a monumental challenge. And frankly, I'm torn and confused. What am I going to do? I can stay. Or I can leave. My entire future hinges on that one decision.

You don't have to be so melodramatic, Howard says. To be completely honest, I always saw you as a bit of a lightweight. One glass of Pinot and you'd be looking for the leitmotif in Abba's lyrics. Are you sure you even have a problem?

You think I *want* to be here?! I say. I can feel The Fury stirring, and I fight it.

In some types of drama, you can be your own Antagonist, and the Lead Character is often portrayed as his own worst enemy. But that's too subtle for most people, particularly in the Flyover States, so I tend to avoid that type of thing. Also, frankly, it's a little precious for my taste.

Guys! Nigel says. Come on. Chill. We're all friends here.

Right! I think. *Friends who are owed money.*

I calm down and we spend a few minutes talking about mundane things. The War in Iraq. (Or is it Iran? I can never get it straight. Maybe it's both by now.) What the confirmation of Alito is going to mean for the country. Karl Rove's astonishing, Teflon-like ability to avoid prosecution. The real estate bubble—Fact or Fiction?

Finally, my so-called friends go on their way. A wave of relief sweeps over me. I walk back to my room and glance at the books, looking for a Hidden Meaning, but my eyes are tired, and I fall asleep.

The next few days are dull.

It

Is

Hard

To

Find

Anything

Interesting

To

Say

So I Must

  Find

    Creative Ways

        To Pad Pad Pad.

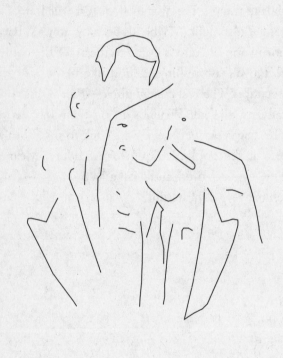

Or maybe semi-creative.

Or maybe not creative at all.

Chuck stops by to remind me to put something on the Goal Board.

What's the Goal Board?

It's in The Lounge. Write your name across the top of a three-by-five card and tell the rest of us your hopes and dreams. What being here means to you.

Means to me how?

Like who you want to be when you walk out of here.

I want to be Brad Pitt.

I hope you are being funny.

I don't understand why that would be funny. Who *wouldn't* want to be Brad Pitt?

I go to another in a series of endless lectures, one more unbelievable than the next. A guy who looks like Steve Buscemi is at the podium, in tears. He had a Great Life, he says. He sold cars for Saturn. (That's a Great Life? Selling cars for Saturn? All right, buddy. If you say so.) He was Employee of the Month three months *in a row*. (Emphasis his.) He and his wife had been trying to have a baby for years and years, and suddenly, thanks to the Miracle of Science, they had four of them—on the same day. Yes, quadruplets. It was really exhausting, as you can imagine. The kids were so fucking *needy*. He fell apart. He and his wife were constantly at each other. He began to go to strip clubs after work, and to drink heavily, and he lost his resolve and slept with hookers, in all shapes, sizes, and denominations. Then he fell in love with one of the hookers, a mere child called Maggie. He thought he could save Maggie, so he left his wife and his four lovely children, and he tried to redeem Maggie, with limited success. In the course of the divorce, Steve Buscemi's wife had several meetings with a bald gentleman who was doing the forensic audit, determined to take Steve for every penny he had, including a portion of his pension plan, and the wife fell in love with the bald gentleman. She got everything, including the gentleman and the four kids. Steve got nothing, unless you count those two restraining orders—one from his estranged wife, the other from Maggie. But wait. The story gets even better: The bald gentleman dies, but luckily he is very organized and all the papers are in perfect order, and he had an excellent Life Insurance policy. Then one day the Wife is at Bloomingdale's— for the bi-annual White Sale—and she is having a hell of a time with the kids. She begins to cry. A woman comes over to help her. Yes, it's Maggie, the hooker. Or *reformed* hooker, I should say. (She has found God.) Maggie not only helps her get the kids under control, but takes the entire family to the Food Court and treats them to pizza and lemonade. (In return, they have to listen to a long, boring story about Moses and the Ten Commandments, which she claims were originally *Fourteen* Commandments, but which God in his Infinite Wisdom realized were about Four More than Most People could handle.) In the end, Maggie and the Wife end up together. They are lesbians and they are pillars of the community, something that only a few years ago would have been Unthinkable, and Steve Buscemi is left with nothing, not even his dignity, Until Now. Until He Found Sleepy Hollow.

A brief question-and-answer period follows.

Did you see the movie *Bound*?

I did not, Steve says.

It's a good movie. Has some interesting similarities.

Another man asks, Is that rumor true about one of the brothers who directed that movie?

What rumor?

Another man raises his hand. How much is a hooker these days?

It depends on what you want.

Just, you know, regular.

It varies. Anywhere from twenty to five hundred.

What do you get for twenty?

Not much.

Do you use a condom?

Of course.

How do you manage to remain erect when you're putting it on?

After the lecture, I head for The Lounge. It occurs to me that the reason I don't enjoy these lectures is because nothing in the world is as interesting to me as my own mind. Maybe that's part of the problem. The other reason I don't enjoy them is that I am tired of all the pious bullshit. I mean, who are these people kidding? Am I the Last Honest Man in America? Maybe I am. I am a Truth Teller, always have been and always will be, and the only question now is how do I turn that into a Work of Artistic Merit?

When I get to The Lounge, I find the usual Needy Losers hanging around. A couple of guys are playing pool. Some are playing cards. A few are watching *Entertainment Tonight* on TV. I drop into the big chair near the bookcases, and I look at the distant TV. I can't hear anything from this distance, but I see a shot of the *real* Angelina Jolie leaving a restaurant with Brad Pitt. She is pregnant with his baby, and she is showing, and when I see her cute little belly I am almost reduced to tears. I don't know why I feel like crying. Am I crying for me, or am I crying for Jennifer Aniston?

I wish it were three o'clock and *Attika* was on. I love the way that show opens. The moment Attika appears on stage, the men and (mostly) women jump to their feet, fists clenched, chanting, At-ti-ka! At-ti-ka! At-ti-ka! It makes the hair stand up on the back of my neck. Every hair. Standing up. Electric blue.

Then some guy changes the channel, and there's a baseball game on, and I remember going to Shea Stadium as a kid, with my father and my brother, Geppetto. Man, I *lived* for baseball season! Walking into that crowded, noisy stadium, my little hand in my father's big hand. Finding our seats. Eating hot dogs and popcorn till I was fit to burst. Feeling lousy, frankly, and climbing into my father's lap to get away from the

stench of spilled beer and stale popcorn and from the
fat, sweaty Neanderthals in the surrounding seats. As I
sat there, pressing my ears to my father's chest (well,
one of my ears, anyway) to drown out the noise, I
would listen to the confident beating of his heart, and
I would hold my breath until our hearts were beating
in unison—two hearts, beating as one. God how I
loved my Father!

Wait a minute? Was that even me? No, I think that was
Jeffrey S., from fourth grade. His father actually had
time for him. My father *never* took me to a baseball
game. I know absolutely nothing about sports, and to
this day I don't understand their appeal.

I turn away from the television. There are a bunch of
dog-eared books on the shelf closest to me. Normally
I would tell you that there are about forty books on
each shelf, and that there are seven shelves, which adds
up to about four hundred books, and I would actually
do some padding by reading off thirty or forty titles,
but I am exhausted by my own overwriting. I still
have to name a few books, however, but I promise to
keep it short: I will only refer to titles that will in some
way service the story. I see a copy of *Dianetics*, but I
don't touch it. Those people frighten me. I see a copy
of something called *Zen Mind, Beginner's Mind*, and I
flip it open at random. "When you try to understand
everything, you will not understand anything. The
best way is to understand yourself, and then you will
understand everything." Well, pal, I think, I can't even

begin to understand *you*. Plus you worry me. That kind of Cheap Philosophy is as addictive as Pinot Noir, and much less satisfying.

I see the Holy Bible, and I am not going anywhere near that. There is no God. There is no Higher Power. I do what I do because of who I am and partly because of genetics, not because Some Egomaniacal Fuck With a White Beard is watching over me and pulling strings like a Cosmic Puppeteer or something. Then I see a tiny little book tucked into the corner. I reach for it. It's called Harrap's Hungarian Phrase Book. This strikes me as another one of life's odd coincidences. Didn't my father say he was on the phone to a Hungarian gentleman in Caracas? What am I going to learn from this book? *Ne nevettesse ki magát*. What an odd language! Every word sounds like a cry for help! I put it down. I see a copy of Dale Carnegie's *How to Win Friends and Influence People*. This one is super dog-eared. I guess a lot of the guys in this place are looking for new friends, having successfully alienated all of the old ones. I flip through the book. Apparently, the secret to friendship and success boils down to bullshit and lies. You should never be honest with people. You should never criticize them. You should never say anything that might be hurtful. No no no. You must be accommodating and pleasant at all times, and you must Act Like You Give a Shit. Apparently, I've been living my life all wrong. I have never been anything less than honest because it's all I know. And if that means having no friends, that's a small price to pay. I have my Integrity. And My Integrity is My Friend.

Then again, maybe we all have a little bullshit in us. Didn't I smile falsely when I saw Howard and Nigel in the Visitor's Area? Didn't I tell them it was nice to see them? I wonder if lying is this kind of Darwinian survival thing that's programmed into us from when we were slugs in the primordial slime. I know it is in Los Angeles, but I didn't think it was universal.

A guy I don't know asks me to play Scrabble with him. He is wearing a bandanna and jeans and a black T-shirt, and he has a nasty scar down the length of his right cheek. He looks and sounds a little like Tony Montana. He stares at me and I stare back until he gets The Message and *knows* that I Am Not To Be Fucked With. He seems appropriately cowed.

We begin to play Scrabble. We choose our letters from the little felt bag, to determine who starts, and he pulls an A. This strikes me as odd, and I wonder if he palmed the tile before we sat down, but I don't say anything.

The first word he puts down is *AINK*.

What is that? I say. That's not a word.

It is dee sound a pig makes, he says in his strange accent.

No it's not. *Dee* sound a pig makes is OINK. With an O.

Not from dee place I call home.

Yeah? What is *dee place you call home*?

New Mexico. He says it like the X is an H, so clearly he has a serious language problem.

The pigs in New Me-*hee*-co say AINK?

Are you fucking with me, man?

I could kill this guy. I am a brown belt in Krav Maga, even though I am not Jewish (or at least I don't *think* I am), but I decide it isn't worth it.

I'm sorry, I say. I can't play Scrabble with a man who thinks a pig says AINK.

Do you want to meet my seester? he asks me.

I laugh my seal-like bark.

You think that ees funny?

No. I don't think that ees funny. Sometimes I just laugh when I'm uncomfortable.

And the truth is, I *am* uncomfortable. I wouldn't mind meeting his sister. I knew a girl called Bilharzia once who was very hot, and I've always had a soft spot for Hispanic women, especially if they don't charge too much. But what if he's messing with me? I decide he is messing with me.

No, thank you, I say. I'm sure your sister ees very nice, but I don't want to meet her.

What's the matter? You think you are too good for my seester?

No no. Not at all. It's just that I'm engaged. And I'm getting married as soon as I get well.

He looks at me like he doesn't believe me. I'm a terrible liar, unless I put my mind to it.

I go back to the big chair, alone with my thoughts, and I realize I have learned a valuable lesson, and the lesson is that people hear things very differently. I hear oink, he hears aink. Perception is not an exact science, unless you're an optician. Every person has his own version of reality.

Then I remember about the Goal Board. I walk across the room, find a three-by-five card, and write my first name and last initial across the top. Under that I write, I WANT TO BE ON ATTIKA SOME DAY. I don't want to hide it anymore, and it seems as if some of the people here already have suspicions about my Literary Aspirations. I know what I want and now I want the world to know it, too. Yes, that is my dream. It is a Big Dream, maybe even an Impossible Dream, but that's what life is all about, isn't it? Dreaming the Impossible Dream.

And I'll tell you this, if it happens, if I ever do get on *Attika*, you won't see me pulling a Jonathan Franzen. I will be grateful and I will cry cry cry. Because ask yourself this, Where is Jonathan Franzen now? I wouldn't be surprised if he ends up on *Hollywood Squares*. With Dave Eggers.

As I pin my card to the corkboard, I read some of the other hopes and dreams. They strike me as incredibly pedestrian.

I WANT TO BE RICH AND HAPPY AND LIVE FOREVER WITHOUT PAIN.

I WANT TO HAVE CHILDREN.

I WANT TO LEARN TO LAUGH AGAIN.

I WANT A BIGGER PENIS.

I WANT TO BE AN AMERICAN HERO: A GOOD HUSBAND, A GOOD FATHER, AND A GOOD MAN.

Oh please!

One of the entries says, I WANT TO BE A BEAUTI-FUL WOMAN.

I think I know who this guy is. This is the short, homely guy who came up to me on my very first day, stopped me in the corridor, and asked, Do you think there's anything wrong with two grown men sitting in a warm tub of water shaving each other's backs?

I said No, but I do think there's something wrong with it.

As I am poring over other Goal Cards—I WANT TO MEET A GIRL WHO HAS THE COURAGE TO PUT HER REAL PICTURE ON MATCH. COM—Lorraine walks in, with Mort close behind. She looks very upset. She tells me—in front of the whole lounge—that she has just looked at the rest-room, and that it is FILTHY FILTHY FILTHY.

Everyone has a job to do at Sleepy Hollow, she says, and we have Rules, and you are not doing your job.

You are wrong, I say. If it is filthy, somebody else made it FILTHY. Because when I left it this morning, it was IM-MA-CU-LATE.

I am trying to like you, Jimmy, Lorraine says. But you are making it very hard. I am trying to like you and to trust you. I know and trust Mort, and I like him less than I like you, and in a completely different, unambiguous way, but you are going to have to work harder if you want to get along here, with the Sleepy Hollow Family. Otherwise, I will be forced to ask you to leave.

"And so help goes away again, having helped in nothing," I say.

What is that?

Nothing, A line from Kafka.

You think that makes you special? That you can quote Kafka from memory? You think it makes you sound *smart*?

No.

It doesn't.

I cleaned the toilets, I repeat. I was proud of my work.

How well do you really know Mort? He did a Darth Vader impression the other day, and it was pretty good, but it made me wonder whether he's all there.

I look up and notice that Mort's left eye is twitching. He reminds me of the Inspector in the Pink Panther series.

I expect more from you, Jimmy, Lorraine says. Much more. Please don't disappoint me. She turns on her heels, smartly, and marches out of the room.

Mort gives me this sort of femme fatale look—I'm thinking Sharon Stone in *Basic Instinct*—then exits, somewhat less smartly that Lorraine. The moment he leaves, the rest of the guys in The Lounge make fun of me, mimicking Lorraine:

I'm trying to like you, Jimmy!

We have rules, Jimmy!

You're FILTHY, Jimmy—FILTHY FILTHY FILTHY!

I bark like a seal and leave the room.

At lunch, I take the meatloaf, which is coated with that phlegmy stuff you sometimes find around the edges of meatloaf that has been prepared with inferior ingredients.

Prepared

With

Inferior

Ingredients

I scrape it off with my fork, and move it to the far side of the plate, but when I take that first bite I see that the meatloaf is actually pretty good and tastes deeply of beef, which should come as no surprise. It reminds me of Home. My mother used to make meatloaf for us once a week, every Sunday night, back in the days when we were A Real Family. We were happy. We did a lot of Family Stuff in those days. Until the troubles began. I know I hurt them. And because I can't think of a better segue, I must tell you that I myself now feel hurt by Mort, and in particular by his lies about the condition of the Group Toilets. I am trying my best to make it here, with my New Temporary Family, and it is hard. Every minute of every day is hard. Hard as hell. I want to drink Pinot Noir, and I want to dance, and I think about drinking and dancing every goddamn day.

Every

Goddamn

Day

Suddenly I see Angelina again, way over on the far side of the room. She is staring at me with such intensity that I am forced to look away. She reminds me of a girl from Connecticut I slept with once. She was rich, a Blue Blood, part of the horsy set. We met in a bar in Manhattan, on the Upper East Side, and she wasn't beautiful in the traditional sense, but she had an intensity about her—especially around the eyes—that I found hard to resist. (That and the wine, I guess, and the fact that it was Almost Closing Time.) She had a pied-a-terre that was walking distance from the bar, and when she asked me if I wanted to stop by for a nightcap, my heart was pounding so hard I thought it would explode through my chest. When we got back to her place, where the walls were covered with pictures of horses, and with the many ribbons she has won, or bought someplace, for show, she slipped into something more comfortable. As she moved toward me, smiling intently, I noticed that her legs were like veritable oaken timbers, and I was a little frightened. But she was both aggressive and persistent, and we managed to do a semi-flaccid version of The Beast With Two Backs.

The last thing I remember, before blacking out, was feeling the weight of those massive legs as they en-

veloped my entire body. I had to visit my chiropractor
four times before I was able to walk fully upright again.

You're getting a little ripe, Benny says.

Excuse me?

The bandage on your ear. You need to get it changed.

Say hi to J. Lo, Larry says.

J. Lo?

The nurse, he explains. Check out that generous ass. It
looks very hot in that white outfit.

After lunch, I go to the infirmary, and the Kindly
Nurse changes the bandage. She looks *nothing* like
J. Lo. She looks like one of those women who hasn't
had a date in forty years and likes small dogs.

When she removes the bandage from my ear, her
eyes Go Wide with Utter Horror, and she literally recoils.

Oh dear, she says.

Is it bad?

No, she says, smiling pleasantly. It occurs to me that
maybe she has read Dale Carnegie.

She cleans the ear, with alcohol, and it stings like hell.
It Stings Worse than Any Sting Anyone Has Ever Felt
in His Life, except for maybe a pirate getting thirty
lashes for some minor infraction. But that was a long
time ago.

Have you looked at your ear? she asks me.

No, I say. How can a person look at his ear?

Use a mirror.

I didn't realize that's what she meant.

No, I say at last, sighing. I have not looked at myself in a mirror in a very long time.

Why not?

I'd rather not talk about it.

All of us are scared, Jimmy. It's natural to be scared. Conversely, to not be scared would be unnatural. You are a good man. I can see that. You need to find a good woman. A woman that completes you.

I wonder if people really talk like that. I guess they do, because I'm not making this up.

There's a mirror across the room, she says, pointing it out. Why don't you have a look at yourself? Why don't you look at the pale green of your eyes, and beyond, at The Man Within, the Real Jimmy, the one who Lives Beneath? Peel back the layers of the onion, Jimmy. The onion may bring tears to your eyes, but they will be like scales, allowing you to See For the First Time—To Truly See!

I thought we had been talking about my ear, but I guess not.

No, I say. *I can't do it. No fucking way. I am not brave enough to look into my own eyes.* I do not want to look into that hole. That hole is deep, and it is black, and I live in it. I am a fucked up sad-sack with no dignity and no hope. I have disgraced myself, and words cannot describe how I feel. Well, *words* can, but I can't.

I go back to the room, crushed and lonely, thinking about Pinot Noir and Dancing.

Bottle.

Drink.

Not drink.

Fight.

Live.

Die.

Fuck God.

Good fuck.

Able was I ere I saw Elba.

Madam I'm Adam.

Cry.

Like.

A little.

Girl.

Now that I'm wearing a fresh bandage, I realize that the bad smell I encountered everywhere in this place was really me. I lie down and reach for one of the books my sham friends brought as so-called gifts.

"When we are in love, we feel completed," I read. "It's as if we have been reunited with a missing part of ourselves."

That is uncanny! Wasn't the Kindly Nurse just talking about the same thing? I think about this deeply, or as deeply as possible, in my case.

The fact is—and let me hammer this home here, because it speaks to the commonality of human experience—*I don't want to be alone.* I mean, you know what it's like. You go through all the names on your cell phone, A to Z, and you can't find a Single Person Who Understands You. Four hundred and seventeen names, and the only one that even comes close to being a True Good Friend is the person who cuts your hair.

Every time I look through that list, which I do obsessively, sometimes five or six times a day, I feel more alone than ever. I have no one to hold my hand. I have no one to tell me that everything is going to be all right. Where did my hopes and dreams go? I am So Alone.

So

Fucking

Alone

Is there a woman out there for me who can Kill My Loneliness?

Please Say Yes.

Please Make It End.

Doesn't ANYONE OUT THERE HEAR ME SCREAMING?

I wonder if there is hope for me, or whether Benny was right when he said that LONELINESS IS ABSOLUTE.

At that moment, there is a knock at the window. I look over. It is Angelina. *When I see her, my heart jumps and my hands shake and those things for which there are no words start firing firing firing.*

I can't believe she is taking a chance like this! If she gets caught on the Men's Side of Sleepy Hollow, she will be kicked out for sure. She signals to me, like a mime, which is a little off-putting, frankly, for reasons that will become clearer later, but I recover and cross to the window and open it.

What are you doing here? I say.

I had to see you, she says, and *she smiles a deep smile*.

We could get into trouble, I say.

I know, she says. But some risks in life are worth taking, and this is one of them.

After hearing that, I am forced to Throw Caution to the Wind. I climb out and follow her into the nearby woods. As we make our way along, in silence, we reach two divergent paths, and I wonder if this is a symbol of some kind. The idea of being forced to make a decision leaves me completely paralyzed, but Angelina seems to know her way around, so I simply follow her. I get the feeling that this isn't the first time she has done this, and I find myself simultaneously excited and repelled, and for a moment I think I'm on the verge of learning something Really Important about the Complexity of Love. The moment passes, alas, with me none the wiser for it (as usual).

We reach a lovely clearing, overlooking the lake. I can see two loons in the water, mating—or trying to mate, anyway—and I wonder whether this, too, is a sign. There is a blanket stashed under a tree and Angelina gets it and I help her spread it out on the ground. It is soiled in several spots, but that doesn't automatically mean that Angelina is a bad person.

Tell me about yourself, she says.

My name is Jimmy, I say.

I know that part. Keep going. Skip to the good stuff.

I wish I knew how to skip to the good stuff. Somebody once asked Elmore Leonard how he managed to write such compelling, fast-paced novels, and he said, It's easy. I just leave out the boring bits. But I don't find it all that easy. I feel compelled to include everything, *especially* the boring bits, and even to repeat them at every turn.

I tell her that I had a difficult life. I tell her about the Bumper Cars, and about Little League, and then I tell her about the Girl in High School Who Died. What can you say about a girl who died? Plenty, as it turns out. Like the fact that she was killed by a train on the night we had decided we were going to spend the rest of our lives together.

I still remember how long it took me to get the courage to speak to her—three years, to be precise, three years of fantasizing and obsessing, three years of practicing in front of mirrors—and when I finally managed to address her, in person, it wasn't exactly poetry: *When I see you the World stops.*

Get in line, she said.

Did she really say that? Angelina exclaims. That is so awful!

Yes, she did, I say. But I am nothing if not persistent. When I want something, I become very focused—monomaniacal even. That's why I know I will make it, here, in Sleepy Hollow, and out there, In Life.

What happened to the girl?

Finally, she agreed to see me. I wore her down with my importunity. She was able to get past my Wealth and my Good Looks to the Real Jimmy Inside. It was a Saturday night. I was supposed to pick her up, but I asked her to pick me up because I wanted to show her who was in control. Her family had two cars, a Taurus and an old Renault they got at a police auction. Her mother was out in the Taurus. Is this too much detail?

No, no. Not at all.

Anyway, her mother was out in the Taurus. I think she was going to Wal-Mart—they were out of shampoo. Or was it toothpaste? I think it was shampoo. Did I mention that she had beautiful hair?

No.

She did. So do you, by the way.

So she was coming to pick you up in the Renault?

You pay attention, I say. I like that in a woman. Yes, she was coming to pick me up in the Renault. And she was in a hurry. And when she got the to the railroad tracks, she could see a train coming. But she was so eager to get to my place that she made a dash for it. I pause for effect, then lower my voice and deliver the rest in a funereal tone: She didn't make it.

That it so awful, Angelina says. I am so sorry.

You move on, don't you? Isn't that the Secret of Life? You fall down, you get up. And you learn to do it yourself. Like Maria used to say, *If you want a helping hand, look at the end of your arm.*

Who's Maria?

Nobody.

You are such an inspiration to me, Jimmy. Have you ever thought of writing a book about Your Fascinating Life?

I have, I say, and I smile modestly.

Angelina's eyes well with tears. She fans her eyes with both hands, like girls do, and pulls herself together.

I thought you lived in New York City, she says finally. They have railroad crossings in New York City?

Uh, well—this was, like, senior year in high school. My parents wanted to get me out of town. They sent me to Long Island.

I don't know why I tell her this. The fact is, the story didn't happen exactly that way. The Girl Who Died really did die—that part's true. And she really did get hit by a train. That part's true, also. And it was all terribly tragic. But I didn't really know the Girl Who Died, per se, although I did hit on her a few times, and I know I pissed her off. Pissed off her Boyfriend, too. And I have the tattoo to prove it. But that's neither here nor there. The thing is, her death *spoke* to me, and it became a kind of Symbol of My Longing and My Loneliness, and I used it. Is that so wrong?

I don't explain any of this to Angelina. I slap my forehead and say, Good God! Listen to me! I am sitting here going on and on about myself, and I know absolutely nothing about you!

What would you like to know?

Your name would be a good start.

It's Esther, but everyone thinks I look a little like Angelina Jolie, and a lot of people call me that, so it kind of stuck. But I hate it.

Hate it! But why?! It's a major compliment.

Not really. Whenever people say that, they're really saying you're the Ugly Version of that famous person.

I don't think you are ugly at all!

You don't?

No.

I think her legs are a little hairy, though. I've just really noticed them for the first time, and I wonder if Esther's family is from Europe. Maybe Poland.

I think you're a beautiful girl, I say.

Suddenly I am thinking of another beautiful girl, Julia Roberts, to be specific. I remember seeing a picture of her in *People* magazine, and she was waving at someone, and you could see her hairy armpit. It was overwhelming. I wanted to bury my nose in that pit, but I had to settle for sniffing the picture.

What are you thinking about? Angelina asks me.

Nothing, I say. What are you thinking about?

The Poor Girl Who Died.

I purse my lips and try to look like I'm thinking about her, too, but I can't even remember her name. I guess I look appropriately tortured, though, because Angelina reaches up and gives me a small kiss. It doesn't last long, but I get wood. It is good wood. It is wood that holds much promise.

Why did you stop? I say. That was nice. You don't taste like anyone I know.

What does that mean?

What?

That "taste" thing you said.

I don't know. I think I heard it in a movie once. One of those noir movies.

Is it a bad thing?

Not for me.

You've had an interesting life, she says.

Hey, I say. I've just thought of a joke. Do you want to hear it?

Yes.

How do Polacks play Russian Roulette?

I don't know. How?

They put a bullet in every chamber.

I am bowled over with laughter. I can hardly breathe. But she doesn't find it funny. I pull myself together and try to think of something nice to say. I tell her that she reminds me a little of this girl I was with on the night of the Senior Prom.

She was your date?

Yes, I say, which is a lie, but not a *complete* lie.

What happened was, my parents really wanted me to go to the Senior Prom, but I was such an Outcast, and such a Tough Guy, and so Humiliatingly Unpopular, that I decided not to go. So I got all dressed up, in my Armani tux and everything, and drove off in my mom's car in search of a hooker. I found a skanky little thing and we went back to her place, which smelled like cat urine, or eucalyptus, and we did it on her lumpy pull-out bed. It was a horrible experience. Apparently she had the only working fridge in the complex, and people kept coming by to get their beers and stuff, without even knocking, and I found it very disconcerting. To this day, whenever I'm having sex, I lock the door, even if I'm alone—and sometimes *especially* if I'm alone, which I usually am.

You sound like you had a lot of girlfriends, Angelina says.

No, not a lot, I tell her, and in a rare moment of honesty I think, *That is definitely accurate!*

What about you? I ask.

I haven't had a lot of girlfriends, maybe two or three, but I've had a lot of boyfriends. And I'm talking A LOT.

I am tempted to ask her for details, but I know this is not a good idea. I suffer from retroactive jealousy. I decide to say something seductive, and I almost say, *When I see you the World stops.* But I've used that line before, and—worse—she's heard it. So I say, You are really hot. I am glad I met you. I think you have come into my life at a critical juncture, storywise, anyway.

I am not going to fuck you, Jimmy.

You're not?

No. I have a really good feeling about you, and I don't want to ruin it. If I didn't care, I'd be on you like white on rice.

I wish she didn't care so much. For a few minutes, anyway. But I don't say this.

Seriously, she says. I don't want to ruin it. I have fucked too many guys already. Hell, once, during Spring Break, this guy took me to Killington, to ski, and I must have fucked seventeen of his friends in the space of one weekend. I never even got on the slopes.

I kind of wish she hadn't shared that with me. You don't have to tell a person *everything*. I also think to myself, *I better use a condom*.

Wow, I say, You didn't get to ski at all?

No, she says.

Now the thought of having sex with her is making me a little nervous. Don't get me wrong. I still want her—now more than ever, perhaps. But I don't want to be compared to all these guys she's had. It gives me performance anxiety. And in the interests of Full Disclosure I should probably admit that there have been times in my life when I was not able to achieve an erection. If a girl is patient with me, I get over it, but if she laughs and points at it and calls me names, well—that isn't much fun.

What is that? Angelina is saying. A tattoo?

She moves my watch aside and reads the word on my wrist: Jail?

She doesn't even notice that it's misspelled, which is a relief.

You did time? she asks.

Yes, I say. But I don't want to talk about it now.

I didn't do time, not exactly. And it's weird: The two people in this place, the two people I really care about, Benny and Angelina, have asked me about this tattoo, and it's a measure of my Cowardice that I am unable to tell them the truth. The story is quite simple, really. Remember the Girl Who Died? Remember her Boyfriend? Well, the Boyfriend and his Entourage didn't like me very much, for valid reasons, and they were mean to me every chance they got. They'd sucker punch me in the corridor. Put shit in my locker. Trip me in the cafeteria. I could go on, but let's just say they were TOTAL ASSHOLES, which they were.

Anyway, one day, as I'm coming out of class, the Boyfriend body-slammed me into my locker. And I was carrying this thing that I'd been building in wood-working class, sort of like a sailing ship that didn't come out exactly right, and it fell out of my hands and broke into a million little pieces.

A million little pieces.

A

Million

Little

Pieces

I looked down at this thing that was in A Million Little Pieces, and I thought, That's my life. Those million little pieces on the floor there, those pieces represent my life. That's how badly broken my life is. It is so badly broken it can't be fixed. My life is broken *beyond repair*.

Beyond

Repair

And I started cry-ing. I started to cry cry cry. To cry like a little girl.

Like

A

Little

Girl

And the Boyfriend of the Girl Who Died felt really bad. He could see I was having like a nervous breakdown or something. He could see that he had broken something on the *inside* of me, too. And he apologized, and he helped me pick up the Million Little Pieces, even though they were broken *Beyond Repair*. And that night, to Make Amends, the Boyfriend invited me to his house, and his Entourage was there, as always, and we drank. We did some serious drinking. Some. Serious. Drinking.

And at some point I blacked out.

When I woke up, I was in a Tattoo Parlor, and there was this crazy Puerto Rican Kid who smelled of garlic putting a tattoo on my wrist. And he was just finishing up, looking real proud of himself.

And I said, What the fuck?!

And after I hurled, I again looked down at my wrist in disbelief. And then I looked at him and said, again, What the fuck?! What did you do to me? Is that, like, a permanent tattoo or something?

He nodded.

Who the fuck told you to give me a tattoo?!

Your friends.

My friends!

Yes, your friends told me to give you that tattoo.

My friends told you to give me that tattoo?

Why do you repeat everything I say? Do you have echolalia or something?

I hurled again.

I can't believe this, I say, wiping my mouth with the back on my non-tattooed wrist.

What does that mean? J-I-A-L.

I don't know. All I know is that they wanted you to see it all the time. Get it? When you go to look at the time, at your watch, there it is. J-I-A-L.

I couldn't believe it. I walked out of there in shock and hurled again.

The next day, at school, I ran into the Boyfriend and his Entourage. And they were like, Hey! How do you like your tattoo, Jimmy?

I don't, I said. This really sucks. What am I going to do when my parents see it?

Don't you want to know what it means?

Yes, I said. What does it mean?

It means, Jimmy Is A Loser.

Man, that hurt. I cried. I cried big-time. But I didn't want them to see me cry, so I cried in the bathroom. I knew I wasn't a loser, but it still hurt that they would write that on my wrist.

Jimmy?

I look up. Angelina is studying me with concern. Where were you? Where did you go just now? You looked so sad.

Nowhere, I say. It's nothing. I was just thinking.

I really like you, Jimmy. I have a feeling that good things are in store for us.

I hope so, I said.

For a moment, I remember the day my mother took me to this laser place to have the tattoo removed. It hurt like hell. Even with the topical anesthetic, it still hurt like hell, so I wouldn't let them do it. I decided I would rather live with humiliation, even if it meant not checking the time very often, and even it *that* meant that I would be chronically late to everything. Still, it was better than living with pain. Pain was not my friend.

I look over at Angelina again and try not to cry. She is so beautiful. *My heart starts beating like a Cannon on a Field of War.*

I wouldn't think less of you if you went down on me, I say. I could really use a little lovin'. I don't know why I sound like I'm from Texas. Then I remember that my father sounds like he's from Texas whenever he pretends to care, and I see that genetics is truly more powerful than I ever imagined.

No, Jimmy. Be patient. It will be worth it.

I am so fucking horny.

So

Fucking

Horny

I wonder if she likes it from behind. I wonder if she'll let me spank her, lightly at first, and then harder as I get to know her better—with genuine rage. I wonder what she'll say when I ask her, Who's Your Daddy? I wonder if anyone has ever asked her that before while he was fucking her from behind, slapping her ass, and I think the answer to that is a Resounding Yes.

I want you so bad, I say.

I know, Jimmy. And I want you, too. But listen to me, because this is important. If I give myself to you—

If?

When I give myself to you, which will be soon, I want you to know that I am one of those women who Gives Herself Totally. Do you understand what I'm saying?

I think so.

There are no half-measures with me.

Me neither.

When I love someone, I love them completely, with all my heart and soul. Does that frighten you?

No. Should it?

Maybe a little.

I don't care. I think it's worth it.

I hope you remember that down the line. Because if I give myself to you, it's For Fucking Ever. Are you listening to me?

I hear you Loud and Clear.

I don't like goodbyes, Jimmy. When I love, I Really Love.

You say that like it's a bad thing. It's not a bad thing. I've been reading all about love in my new book, *Love Me Tender, Love Me Raw*.

I read that book! I loved that book!

I'm loving it, too! It is so interesting! I love all that wonderful stuff about "being overtaken by love's mysterious power." How love lifts you above "the ordinary plain of human existence." How the Ultimate Meaning of Life is revealed to you through your love for This Other Person That You Love.

I remember that last part! she exults. The one about the Ultimate Meaning. I *loved* that part!

I want to Feel Whole with you, Angelina. I think we can complement and complete each other, like it says in the book.

Well, keep reading, she says. Nine out of ten times, you end up wanting to kill the person You Thought You Loved.

I don't care, I say. I know what I feel.

Jesus, I've got some serious wood. If I just threw her down on the blanket right now I *know* I wouldn't have performance anxiety, but I can't do that. It's not right. I'm not saying it's not not right always, but this time, in this particular situation, with all the promise that it holds, it's definitely not right.

Whoever said there was no escape from human solitude—and I think it was more than one person— was wrong. Dead wrong. I am looking at My Escape right now, and She Is Hot.

She

Is

Fucking

Hot

Whoever said there was no such thing as Love at First Sight was also wrong; dead wrong. Plus they don't understand the meaning of Dramatic License.

We better go, she says. We don't want to be missed.

I'll be missing you every second of every minute of every hour until I see you again, I say. I think this is a pretty good line, and she does too, apparently.

I must really like you, she says. That thing you just said—it sounded like poetry.

We run back through the woods, not talking, not wanting to spoil it with unnecessary verbiage, and part ways.

That night, I dream I am at a wine tasting. Everyone is spitting out their wine, except me. These are high-end Burgundies. They are too good to waste. I get really blotto.

As the dream continues, I am running naked through a vineyard, reaching for the plump grapes and stuffing them in my nose.

Kill what hurts. Kill it. Kill my heart. Kill my mind.

Kill kill kill.

My own voice wakes me up.

Kill kill kill.

But I don't sound like myself.

I sound very nasal.

Honk! Honk! Honk!

I feel like I have grapes in my nose. I check. I *do* have grapes in my nose!

Either Life is Incredibly Mysterious, or some asshole in this place has a really sick sense of humor.

5.

I get out of bed, even though it is only six in the morning, and I brush my teeth, shave, and wash my face, all without looking myself in the eye. I feel a lot better about things—especially with Angelina in my life—but I'm not a hundred percent there yet, and I don't want to screw everything up by seeing something in myself that I would have been better off not seeing.

I make my way over to the Group Toilets and really clean them this time. I scrub and scour until my hands are red and raw, like the inside of a chicken that hasn't been cooked properly. When I'm done, I stand there with my fists on my hips, admiring my work. I walk the length of the sinks, and then I inspect the stalls one more time, and I am pretty impressed with myself. I feel a little proud, if you want to know the truth. It must be true what they say: Good work molds the spirit.

By this time, breakfast is being served, so I head off to eat. I am hungry as a horse again. Part of it is related to the Emptiness Within, but part of it is related to the sheer joy of doing hard, honest work.

I walk into the Mess Hall and look around for Angelina. I do not see her, but I see several Crack Ho–types at one of the tables checking me out and whispering amongst themselves. I hope Angelina hasn't been indiscreet; I hope she hasn't said anything about our Romance; mostly I hope I'm not just being paranoid. I went through a paranoid phase once, and it was not pleasant. Especially for my father's secretary.

There is some good eatin' today. I pile on the French toast, four pancakes, a mess o' scrambled eggs, bacon, and sausage, and then I reach for a roll. The roll is as hard as a rock. I hold it aloft, in a pseudo-Biblical pose, and intone loudly, "Who among you, if asked for bread, would give me a stone?" This is not an original line. It is something the poet Delmore Schwartz once said, in a rare moment of levity, for him, anyway, and it seems as if I have been waiting my whole life to use it. The result is somewhat less than expected. People are looking at me like I'm a lunatic. I know there is a lesson in this somewhere, but I don't know what it is.

I bark like a seal, reach the end of the line, pour voluminous amounts of maple syrup over my entire meal, including the eggs, and join the guys at the Cool Table, where I proceed to shovel the food into my mouth like a caveman. I know the guys are watching me, but I don't care. I'm in love, and when you're in love you feel you can do anything!

Benny is next to me. He starts to cough, a phlegmy, cringe-inducing cough, and he just keeps coughing, so Larry pounds him on the back. Benny turns and slaps him.

Hey, Larry says. I was just trying to help!

I can take care of myself, Benny says, wheezing, and he begins to cough again. It sounds awful, like a harbinger of worse to come, and I want to say something nice to Benny, something pleasant, but I don't have it in me. I'm just not that comfortable around illness or death, impending and otherwise.

So I ignore him and look around the Women's Side of the Room, hoping for a glimpse of my Inamorata. The women seem to be divided by Socioeconomic Class, and Angelina is definitely in the Lowest Class, so I look toward that side of the room. Nothing. I wonder where she is. I wonder if she's all right. I wonder if she's shaving her legs. That would be good.

I am still hungry. The Food Only Kills the Need Momentarily. I am smart enough to know this, but what good does it do me? Just because you understand gravity—which I don't—doesn't mean that you have conquered it.

Benny stops coughing, and in the relative silence that ensues I can hear the other guys talking about the Enron Trial, Kelly Clarkson's tearful appearance at the Grammys, that poor son of a bitch that got shot by Dick Cheney, the miraculous transformation in Britney Spears since she became a mother, and the

Bush administration's shameless position on wiretaps, which is specious at best. I make a mental note to myself to try to keep abreast of current events, but the word "abreast" makes me realize that I am still enormously hungry. I remember walking past some huge cinnamon buns in the food line, with raisins right where the nipples would be, and I decide to pick up two or three. Just as I am about to get to my feet, however, Benny turns and looks at me in a conspiratorial manner.

Watch yourself, kid, he says, whispering.

I'm not sure I heard him correctly.

What's that?

He comes closer, because he doesn't want the other men to hear.

I can understand the attraction, he says. But try not to get in too deep.

What are you talking about? I ask him.

Who am I talking about, he says, correcting me. Then he adds, I think you know the answer to that, Jimmy.

I don't know what to say. Is my friend Benny talking about Angelina? How does he know about her? And what does he mean about getting *in too deep*?

Don't look so worried, he says, still whispering. I'm just telling you to watch your step, because in the short time I've known you, I've begun to think of you as my own son. I like you, Jimmy, and I wouldn't want to see you get kicked out before you're ready to face the world. Then he gives me a little nudge, a sweet, pater-

nal gesture, and adds, You got good taste. I'll say that
for you.

Thanks, I say.

Just then, I see Lorraine hurrying toward our table.
She doesn't seem to be in a very good mood. I wonder if this is connected to Angelina, and if it explains
her absence this morning, and suddenly I am pretty
nervous.

I need you to come with me right away, Lorraine says.

W—what's wrong? I say.

You'll see.

I get up and follow her out. I can feel everyone
watching us, curious, and I am worried. I have never
been comfortable in the limelight.

We walk down the corridor, and people follow behind
us, excited. Nobody knows what the hell is going on,
but they know it's Big.

Lorraine leads the way into the Group Toilets, gestures
theatrically, like Vanna White, and says (loudly enough
to be heard by the growing crowd in the corridor), Do
you call this clean?

I look around. The place looks like it's been hit by a
tornado, for want of a better cliché.

No, I say. This is not clean. But when I was done here,
not an hour ago, it was sparkling. This is a deliberate
act of sabotage, by Someone Who Does Not Like Me.
I look up. Mort is standing near the half-open door,
smirking, but when Lorraine turns in his direction the
smirk quickly disappears and is replaced by an almost

paternal look of disappointment. I have seen that look many times in my young life, and it just sets me off. I dive for Mort, and we go sailing through the door and into the corridor, where the crowd parts and forms a circle to watch The Fury in action.

Lorraine tries to stop us, but there is no stopping me. I am A Man Possessed.

A

Man

Possessed

I have my powerful hands clamped around Mort's throat, and I am squeezing the life out of him, and his Adam's apple bobs like a skittish mouse. *I can feel my blood moving through my veins.* I am ready to kill. I do not mind killing. If I kill him, it really isn't me; it's The Fury. The Fury did it. I'll be able to compartmentalize the incident. In years to come, whenever people speak about Mort's Brutal Murder, I will genuinely not know what the fuck they're talking about. But something inside me—a Basic Goodness I am unable to deny, or a Voice, or the thought of being in a prison for real and having to be Some Guy's Wife—tells me not kill Mort. As I said earlier, good drama doesn't tell you a man's entire life; it takes an incident in his life and reveals What He Is All About through his handling of said incident. This is what they call a Defining Moment, and this is one such moment for me. I am better than this.

I. Am. Better. Than. This.

I
Am
Better
Than
This
I loosen my grip on Mort's throat, and I get to my
feet, with the blood still roaring in my ears—or my
ear-and-a-half, anyway. As the roaring abates, I can
hear the restive crowd all around me, but I don't hear
what they say—except for one tasteless comment
about my socks—because I am staring intently at
Mort. He is gasping like a landed fish, or like a man
who hasn't taken a deep breath in a long time, or both,
and when I look at him I do so because I want him to
know that I have spared his life.
I
Have
Spared
His
Life
For a moment, I am reminded of that Asshole who
broke my little wooden sailboat, but I know that Mort
is not him, although now that I think about it he does
look like a little bit like him, and I wonder if perhaps I
should make him him. There are always outrageous
coincidences in stories of this type, but people get over
them: if they didn't, there would be no point in going
to the movies. And now that I think about it, I wonder
if perhaps *that's* the reason people have *stopped* going

to movies: because most of them suck. To be honest, I stopped going to movies after I saw *Into the Blue*. That was a new low, and it *didn't have to be*. They could have done something really intelligent with that film, but no—they went out of their way to make it Really Fucking Stupid.

What is wrong with me? I think. I don't think this because I almost killed a man. I think it because my mind goes off on all these crazy tangents that have nothing to do with anything. I don't know what's real anymore, and I'm beginning to think it doesn't really matter. If something feels real, it *is* real. Like the bugs I saw crawling on the walls the first night I was here. If they weren't real, why did I spend half the night smashing them with the palm of my hand, and the other half of the night washing my hands compulsively? Explain that to me.

Mort is on his feet now, still panting, leaning against the wall for support. Two of the Black Guys in White push their way through the crowd, but they can see the worst is over, and they can also see that Mort is about to say something portentous and meaningful. The place is deathly still.

I'm listening, I say.

I notice Lorraine out of the corner of my eye, also listening.

I'm sorry, man. Mort says. I lied. That bathroom was clean. That bathroom was so clean I hated you for it. I wanted to bring you down. I don't know why. It seems like you've been given every advantage in the world, and I've been given nothing.

I roll my eyes. Here it comes. *The Great American Sob Story.* This place is full of them. This place is crawling with wimps who refuse to take responsibility for their actions. When are you going to learn, people?! You are doing this to *yourselves*! When are you going to stop blaming blaming blaming?!

When my sailboat broke into A Million Little Pieces, I didn't sit there and cry. (Or maybe I did, a little.) I went out to Blockbuster and rented *Beaches* again, for the third time, and it helped put my life into context, *again*. And, yes, I cried like a little girl at the end of the movie. But then I did what had to be done. I dried my tears, people. I dried my own fucking tears. Nobody dried my tears for me. Not that night, not ever. So don't talk to me about pain and misery. I understand pain and misery. Pain and misery are my middle name(s).

That's it, Mort? You call that an apology? That's the best you can do?

Suddenly Mort's eyes go all funny. He seems possessed. All right, Mr. DeMille, he says in a woman's voice, and it is a voice I recognize only too well.

I'm ready for my close-up.

This is not funny, people. You know what it is? It's fucking heart-breaking.

Lorraine crosses to Mort's side.

With everyone watching in stunned silence, she takes him gently by the fleshy upper arm and begins to lead him away.

All right, Miss Desmond, she says. Let's go.

Are they ready for me now, Mr. DeMille? Mort says in that same breathy voice.

Yes they are, Miss Desmond.

How do I look?

You have never looked lovelier.

I feel like crying. Lorraine movies past, guiding Mort along, and she whispers to me, I will see you in my office later, after I deal with this. I'm afraid I owe you an apology.

I am thinking, *Yes you do, bitch*. But I gleaned a little something from that cursory reading of Dale Carnegie, so I say, simply, Okay. That's cool. Don't worry about it.

Then she moves off, with Mort/Norma at her side, and the crowd parts, just like the Red Sea parted for Moses, but not exactly, because there is no roaring wind, and, come to think of it, no Large Body of Water.

A guy I never liked walks up to me. He looks a little bit like Sean Penn, and he has that same kind of humorlessness about him. He acts like he's better than everyone and smarter than everyone. I'm not saying Sean Penn is like that, mind you, and in fact I don't believe he is; I mean, he can't possibly think he's better than everyone, and if he thinks he's smarter than everyone I'm here to tell him that he's definitely not smarter than me. But you get the idea: this guy has that whole icky Sean Penn thing going on, and it has rubbed me the wrong way from the moment I first laid eyes on him, and I hope he doesn't say anything to set me off, because The Fury is still lurking very near the surface.

He says, I've got to tell you something, man.

What? I say.

As a result of what I saw here today, I have grudging respect for you.

What does that mean—*grudging respect*? I've never understood that phrase (so maybe I'm not as smart as Sean Penn). I don't even know you, I say. How can you grudge me anything?

Hey, man, I don't want to get on your wrong side. I've seen what you are capable off. I'm just trying to say that I respect you. You have the respect of a lot of people in this place. I think that should be pretty clear by now, but we might as well belabor it.

Thank you, I say.

I say that, but I'm not sure I care. What does it mean to have the respect of people you yourself don't respect? Think about *that* for a moment.

That wasn't always the case, Sean Penn is saying. When you first got here, a lot of us weren't sure you were going to make it. On the outside, you're not a guy who inspires immediate confidence. But there is much more to you than meets the eye. And I just wanted you to know that you have nothing left to prove to anyone.

Thanks, I say.

I go to the lecture later, and there's a rumor it's going to be Donald Trump. I don't believe this for a minute, because none of the rumors here ever turn out to be true, but I am sort of excited because I've always been fascinated by Donald Trump, and by his hair, because I, too, am losing my hair, and I am just as desperate to hide it (but not like *that*, for Christ's sake!) Also, a couple of nights ago there was a big thing on Trump on *Access Hollywood*. Apparently a guy had written a book about him claiming that he wasn't worth anywhere near the $2.7 billion dollars he claimed to be worth, and that the figure was closer to a hundred and fifty million dollars, if that. The Donald was suing this poor writer for five billion dollars, for defamation and libel, which seemed a little excessive to me, but the writer was thrilled. Apparently no one had read his book, but now with the lawsuit it was flying off the shelves.

The crack investigative team at *Access Hollywood* also spoke to another writer, a guy who had once had the audacity to do a less-than-fawning profile on Trump. Trump hated the guy so much that he had sent him a note calling him a TOTAL LOSER, and, for good measure, he added that his writing TOTALLY SUCKED. He went out of his way to point out that he, Trump, had read a few *real* writers, like John Updike and Philip Roth and Orhan Pamuk, which I guess was his way of saying that he knew whereof he spoke. I don't know how the writer responded, but that's not the point. The point, once again, is this whole issue of perception, of fact versus fiction. And my question to you is, Who decides? Not just about Trump's net worth, but about the quality of the writing? (I may have to look at this again. I'm not sure I've made my point clearly, and in fact I believe I completely lost my train of thought.)

As it turns out, the lecturer is not Donald Trump, which was never even a remote possibility to begin with. How could it have been? Donald has never been Out of Control. Donald has never had A Problem. Donald can't sing, and Donald can't dance. Need I say more?

Instead of The Donald, we get a guy who turns out to be another weepy loser, as pious as the rest of them. But wouldn't you know it? He has an Amazing Story. Maybe the Most Amazing Story of All. And this is his story:

When he was twelve years old, he was seduced by a nun, and she was hot. But one day, inexplicably, she broke it off with him and left town. He began to drink, and for the next twenty years he lived in an alcoholic haze, and made ends meet by delivering mail, or, more accurately, *miss*-delivering it. One day, he was sitting in his shitty little basement apartment in San Francisco, on a Saturday afternoon, nursing his ninth beer, when he decided that he was going to end it all. He wrote a long, involved suicide note. In this note, he went into great detail about his struggle to Earn his

Value as a Human Being, which he felt was the main self-analytic problem of life. He wanted to be a Good Man, he said, wanted to be Kind and Virtuous and Generous, but that was only during that brief period before the third beer kicked in. The fact is, he knew that he was like All Other Men, that he lied to himself about himself and about the world around him, and that he was just another Fucking Loser with absolutely No Control over his Destiny. (What a cop-out!) Eventually he grew tired of trying to become anything, and tired of lying to himself, and to others, about who he was or about his Place in the Universe. He had come to the conclusion, after maybe ten thousand bottles of beer, and more hangovers than he cared to remember, that people were fundamentally dishonest about reality. We write our own illusions, he concluded. We see only what we want to see. Because to see the world as it really is is more than most human beings can endure.

Jesus, what a fucking bore! Get over it, man, I wanted to shout. You're right! Nobody gives a shit about you. People only care about themselves. *Next!*

Predictably enough, that's when his story took an Incredible Turn. The part-time Postal Worker left his shitty apartment in the late afternoon, squinting into the sinking sun, and somehow made his way to the Golden Gate Bridge. As he began to climb, preparing for the Big Jump into the Big Empty, a passing motorist spotted him, and called the cops. A Young Patrolman was the first on the scene: a fresh-faced kid, barely twenty years old, and—unbelievably enough—this was *his very first day in uniform*. He began trying to talk the guy down. He didn't want to lose somebody on his first day on the job, since that would doubtless color all the days that followed, so he tried to connect with the Unhappy Postal Worker (redundant!) as one human being to another. He decided to talk to him about the only thing he knew: *his own life*. He told him that he became a cop because he wanted to Help People; wanted to Do Good. And he told him that being a cop had made him feel, at long last, as if he Had Found His Place in the World—even though this was only his first real day as a cop, and even though it was already clear to him that many of the rookies were looking forward to becoming corrupted. Then he went on to tell him that Belonging was Important to him, because he had never had a Father of his own, and that his mother was a Useless Stoner who sold pot to make ends meets—yada yada yada. But brace yourselves now, because here comes the so-called good part: The Young Patrolman said, "She wasn't always a bad person, my mother. In fact, at one point, many years ago, she was Such a Good Person that she had given her life over to the Service of God. But she met a guy, and she got pregnant, and, well, things didn't turn out as she had hoped." So you see where we're headed with this crock of shit? The Unhappy Postal Worker is about to jump, and he finds out that the

Young Patrolman is his son! The Postal Worker is only thirty-three years old and he has a twenty-year-old son! How great is that? But wait! There's more. The Defrocked Nun had cleaned up her act. She is older now, yes, and gravity has done unspeakable things to her face and body, but she has that Beautiful Older Woman thing going, which I personally have never seen in *anyone* except Julie Christie and Lauren Hutton. And so she and the Postal Worker are reunited. And that's your fucking story: A useless drunk, on the brink of suicide, finds the family he never knew he had—and a reason to go on living. Yeah, pal. Tell it to Hollywood. If I hear one more inspirational story like that, I will hurl bigger than Linda Blair.

After the lecture, Lorraine is waiting for me, looking solemn, and she takes me into her office and closes the door behind us. This is the first time she has ever closed the door, and it speaks to the portentousness of the situation.

I wanted to apologize for not believing you about Mort, she says.

That's okay, I say, brimming over with magnanimity.

In case you're interested, the poor guy is a real mess. We seem to be dealing with some variant of MPD.

MPD?

Multiple Personality Disorder, she explains. But in Mort's case, his personalities are all connected to film characters, which indicates that his grasp on reality is very tenuous indeed.

I like the way we keep hammering this theme about the nature of reality (without being obvious or over-doing it).

Then Lorraine does a very strange thing. In a pro-nounced, lilting, Southern accent, she says, "What we've got here is a failure to communicate."

We do? I say.

No, no, she says. Mort said that. On his way out, he became Strother Martin in *Cool Hand Luke*.

I hear that was a good movie, I say.

You really should get out more, Jimmy. I know you have a tremendous universe in your head, straining to be released, in book form, but it would be good to get away from it once in a while. It would give you a Bet-ter Grip on Reality.

You're probably right, I say. And I'm proud of myself, because Dale Carnegie says you should never contra-dict anyone, unless it's Donald Rumsfeld or some-thing, which you do at your own risk, and that's why I'm being so goddamn accommodating. Then I re-member another line from Dale Carnegie—*Remember that a person's name is to that person the sweetest and most important sound in any language*—so I quickly add, *Lor-raine.*

She looks at me, and I can see that adding that single word has had an immediate and powerful effect—that Dale Carnegie was right.

I am trying to figure you out, Jimmy, she says. When you first got here, I found you very attractive, and also a little dangerous, but in a good way. How do you feel about that?

I don't know how I feel about that, I say, but the truth is, I don't feel good about it at all.

Lately, she adds, I've begun to feel more maternal toward you. I've met your parents, and they are Fine People, and if they fucked you up it wasn't with malice aforethought. So I'm not saying I want to take their place.

What are you saying?

That I want you to know I'm here for you. That I want you to think of me as a mother, a young, still-sexy mother, albeit a childless mother, and that if it turns into something else, well, so be it.

That's very generous of you, I say. But I don't mean it. It feels kind of wrong to me. Plus I don't think she's all that sexy. If I was fifty-two years old, I'd probably be really excited about the thought of sleeping with her, but I'm not fifty-two, and frankly I don't want to think about her naked.

It's sad, though, she says wistfully. When a woman turns forty—not that I'm there yet—she becomes invisible. Men no longer see her. She can spend hours at home, trying to look her best, and she can work out till her tits disappear, but she's wasting her time.

Is that why so many women over forty look so frumpy? I ask. Because they realize it's a waste of time, and they give up?

Maybe, she says.

I can see I have hurt her feelings, and this sounds like a sexist comment, so I try to recover. I guess aging is hard for everyone, I add. There is nothing more pathetic than a fifty-year-old guy with a pony-tail and hoop earring, huh?

I guess, she says. I don't really think about that. I think mostly about me, and how desperately lonely I am. People keep telling me that friendship is the new romance, but I don't see it. Friendship is overrated. If I have to put that much energy into pretending I'm interested in the person across the table, I might as well get laid for my efforts.

I can see your point, I say.

Listen, she says. There's a Group Therapy Session on the second floor in a few minutes. I'd like you to attend.

I don't like that kind of thing. I don't like talking about myself.

I think it would be good for you. You'll learn a lot. It might get you out of here faster.

The Group Therapy Session is run by a Priest, and he has such a pronounced burr that it's almost impossible to understand what he's saying. I get the impression, however, that the Subject of the Day relates to Making Amends. From what I can tell, he's thinks it's critically important to seek forgiveness and to admit fault, even if you don't feel it. This just strikes me as more bullshit. Why do we lie? Is that what life boils down to? What happens to people like me? Decent men who cannot lie?

I look around at the Other Guys, and they all have *the glazed eyes of the Converted*.

But I am not like them.

I am a man who cannot lie.

I

Cannot

Tell

A

Lie

The Priest looks at me. He says something that sounds like, *Wait air you tanking, mein soon,* which makes no sense to me.

Excuse me? I say.

One of the men next to me, a man who has obviously had previous experience with the Priest, translates into decipherable English. Enunciating very clearly, he says, Father McDermid asked, "What are you thinking, my son?"

Well, I say, and everyone is staring at me, I'm afraid I don't believe in this Amends business. I don't see why I should ask anyone to forgive me. What makes them so special? And I don't think I've done anything so horrible, anyway, if you don't count what happened with the mime. And if I'm wrong, if I have done something horrible, I can't undo it. So what's the point?

Father McDermid asks me something else, which is even more tortured than the previous question, and the Man Who Knows Him Well comes to my rescue once again. Father McDermid asked, "But it's really for you, me dear boy! It's about wiping the slate clean and getting rid of the guilt and starting fresh!"

Guilt? I say. I don't feel any guilt.

The Priest and I get into a long conversation, which is made all the longer by our need for an interpreter, and I finally tell him, point blank, that I don't believe in God. Life just ends, I say. It ends. There is nothing out there. Just blackness. It means nothing. *When you're dead, you're dead. There's no coming back.* You are born, you live, you die. Some people live in a slum in India, some in a co-op on Park Avenue. Some people have fun, some don't. And that's all there is to it. You don't get points for doing good things, and you don't get demerits for doing bad things, because there is nothing else. Period. End of fucking story.

There

Is

Nothing

Else

Father McDermid is quite upset by this, and there are a lot of "me boys" and "me lads," which becoming increasingly heated as we argue back and forth (with the help of the interpreter). Toward the end, Father McDermid is punctuating each word with stabs of the forefinger, and occasional slamming his fist against the desk, and he has gone quite red in the face. Finally he bolts to his feet, apoplectic, and says something that sounds like "Go fuck yourself!" but I don't stick around for the translation (so perhaps I misunderstood, and maybe he was saying, "Bless you, Jimmy. And may the Lord be with you and always guide you toward the Right Path").

Later, when I see Benny and the guys, at the Cool Table, I tell them about Father McDermid, and about how red his face got, and they all laugh. But afterward, Benny says something that gives me pause. He says, You know, Jimbo, most Americans believe in God. This is a very purposeful nation. Americans are always going on about Manifest Destiny and what not. They believe that life has purpose, and direction, and that there *is* a Master Plan.

So?

So, he says, you should think about it. If you're going to write a book about your life, you're going to want those people on your side. Those are the people in the Flyover States, as you refer to them so disparagingly, but they buy books, Jimmy. *They buy books.*

I don't understand, I say. You're telling me to lie to sell books?

You wouldn't be the first, he says.

That's not the point. If I'm not honest about my lack of faith, why should I be honest about anything else? If I lie about that, why shouldn't I lie about *everything*?

You shouldn't lie about everything. Just about the things you need to lie about. It's your show. Turn on the lights that flatter you, Jimmy. Everything else can stay in the dark.

Wow, Benny. I had you figured all wrong.

Why are you making such a big fuss about this?

Because I need to. If I don't have The Truth, I have Nothing.

Benny looks at me like I'm a moron. I hate that. I leave without finishing my dessert.

That night, I dream that I've written a book, and that it's actually been published, though it isn't exactly taking the country by storm. The book is called *Pinot Noir, Mon Amour*. Even in my dream I understand, vaguely, that this is some sort of homage to *Hiroshima Mon Amour*, the Alan Resnais film, but I can't figure out what it means, if anything. I saw the film once, Under the Influence, and I thought I understood it, but The Message eluded me; and I saw it again, sober, and I realized I had understood it better when I was drunk. I think it had something to with getting dumped by someone you love, and how it always feels like the End of the World, but I could be wrong. It may have had something to do with Nuclear War, and the *real* End of the World.

At first—and we're still in my dream here—My Book languishes. But then one day I get a call from a woman who says she works with Attika, My Hero, and she tells me that Attika read the book and loved it. She wants to know if I'm available to appear on her Talk Show.

Am I available? I say in the dream. Are you fucking kidding me?

In the dream, I am immediately transported to the show, and it's like I'm having an Out of Body Experience. I know I am dreaming, but even in the dream I am floating above my own body, looking down at myself, and at Attika, on the same couch where Tom Cruise lost it and declared his love for Katie Holmes (leading everyone to question his sincerity, his sanity, and a couple of other things).

I want you to know that this was one of the most moving memoirs I have read in my entire life, Attika says.

Thank you, I say.

The audience goes fucking insane. Attika looks from left to right and back again, like a Queen, surveying her Queendom, and I wonder what her private life is like. When she gets up in the morning, and brushes her perfect teeth, does she look in the mirror and think, *I am the most powerful Talk Show Host in the Universe.* Or does she pretend she's a regular person? If I had to guess, I would guess the former.

Do you know what I loved most? Attika says. I loved the fact that you did it on your own. That you just went out there and Took Control of Your Life. And I loved that phrase you came up with: *Just hang on!*

The Audience goes nuts. I want to tell Attika that I didn't really come up with that phrase, that My Friend Benny came up with it, but in my dream I am still a little disappointed by Benny, and by his shaky morality, so I don't say anything.

When the largely female audience finally gets itself under control, Attika says, in her firm but dulcet tones, "I urge you to buy this amazing book. It is filled with the most *incredible*, most *unbelievable* stories I have ever read, and I loved every credibility-stretching page of it."

The Book, which has been languishing at Number 207,816 on the Amazon List of Most Popular Titles, suddenly takes off. By the end of the day, it's at Number 32. By the following morning, it's at Number 9. By nightfall, it hits Number One.

I wake up. This isn't a Dancing Dream. It's a Writing Dream. I like Writing Dreams better than Dancing Dreams.

I like it so much that I go back for more.

In Part Two of the Dream, I am at a big party. My publisher, Muffy Talons, is showing me around. She speaks in a soft, breathy voice that seems common among people who grew up with too much money and too much help. She tells everyone that I'm Brilliant and Wonderful and I don't contradict her. We pose for photographers.

A woman that looks like a Dominatrix comes by to congratulate me.

That's a really unbelievable book, she says, holding my hand between both of hers. Really *unbelievable*.

She leaves, abruptly, and as she turns to go I check out her fine ass. I think she has a little tail, like a cute pig, or the Devil, but it's dark and hard to see. Still, this changes everything. Suddenly I don't feel so good. What did the Dominatrix mean by putting so much emphasis on the word *unbelievable?* What was she insinuating?

My Dream has taken a very dark turn indeed. I wish I had stopped while I was ahead.

I want to wake up. I look for the exit so I can get the fuck out of Dream Land, but I can't find the god-damn door.

I know that MY DREAM IS TRYING TO TELL ME SOMETHING, BUT WHAT?

My Dream is Trying to Tell Me Something.

But what?

What

Is

My

Dream

Trying

To

Tell

Me?

I wake up screaming. I wake up screaming and crying. Scream-ing and Cry-ing like a little girl.

Like

A

Little

Girl

6.

In the morning, I go to breakfast and I see Angelina. She looks beautiful. She looks like she's had a thousand dollars' worth of beauty treatments, which still isn't enough, but hey—it's a start. I think I can almost smell her hair from here, but it's only the French Toast. I further notice that the dark circles under her eyes are almost gone, and I think, *Cosmetics have improved by leaps and bounds over the years.*

Angelina indicates her tray with a thrust of the chin. There are three glasses of orange juice on it, and I understand that this is a sign. I am to meet her at our Secret Trysting Place at Three O'clock.

Wait! Is she pointing at her fork? Fork fork fork. Yes! We're going to *fuck.* I know that, and I expect no less. But wait another minute! Hold on. Fork in Spanish is *tenedor.* Maybe she can't wait till three. Maybe she wants to meet at *ten* o'clock. *Ten* from *tenedor,* get it?

No. She is shaking her head from side to side. That can't be it. Much too complicated. I'll go with my gut, which has always served me well. Three O'clock it is!

I reach the Cool Table, excited. Benny is coughing again, an unpleasant, rattling cough, and I feel like I should act concerned, particularly in light of some of those pointers I picked up from Dale Carnegie, but I'm thinking of Angelina, only of Angelina.

When Benny finally gets the coughing under control, he turns to me and says, That was quite the performance yesterday.

What? I say. The way I took Mort down outside the Group Toilets?

No. The Postal Worker. At the lecture.

Oh that! I say. What a crock of shit!

Alan says, You think so? One of the guys in the audience is a Big Producer, and he optioned the story.

What guy?

The one with the beard. The one who looks like a rabbi.

That's weird. I thought he *was* a rabbi.

I believe he was, actually. Long ago. I think something happened.

I don't want to hear another Amazing Story, I say.

It's not that amazing, Benny says. It's really quite simple. It was a Crisis of Faith.

How do you know this? Michael asks.

We talked about it, Benny says. We had a long, boring conversation about the Christian approach to God, versus the Jewish approach, but our lengthy talk was punctuated by moments of real brilliance.

Yeah?

According to the rabbi, the Christians just take whatever God doles out, and they accept it unquestioningly, but the Jews get pissed off. They think they're supposed to hold God accountable for all the bad things that happen, so they talk back to him and clamor for justice.

A lot of fucking good it's done anyone, Larry says.

Well, the rabbi agrees with you there, Benny says. *That* was the crisis. He got tired of clamoring. He moved his family to Hollywood and got into movies.

Movies are the reason we're here, Elliot says.

What do you mean?

Nobody really wants to hear what you have to say, Larry tells Elliot. Larry is mad at Elliot because he had dibs on that seat and Elliot took it anyway.

I don't care, Elliot says. I'm still going to tell you. I have this theory, see. People are always complaining about violence in the movies, but there's nothing wrong with violence. The problem with movies is the way they portray *romance*. We watch these movies, and everyone is beautiful and smells nice, and they all have simultaneous orgasms, and everything always ends happily. Then the music swells, and we're choking back tears, thinking, *That's what I want! Keira Knightley. On her knees. With her hands tied behind her back. Right here*. And of course that monster you've got at home doesn't even look *remotely* like Keira Knightley, and if you so much as *suggest* binding her hands behind her back she's liable to pop you with the fucking frying pan, but that's what you're stuck with, and you know it, and it kills you a little more every day, until finally, one goddamn morning, you wake up screaming.

You know, Larry says. That's the first intelligent thing you've ever said.

Fuck you.

I mean it.

Benny rolls his eyes and turns to me and whispers, So how's your hot girlfriend?

I don't know what you're talking about.

And how's the book coming? I saw you in The Lounge yesterday, scribbling furiously in your little notepad.

I don't get it. It's like Benny sees everything! I look up and Angelina is gone. I turn toward Benny, and I say, whispering, Hey, Benny, you know, with a woman, has it ever happened to you that, you know, you can't?

Never, he says. That's one area where I have never had a problem.

I get nervous sometimes, I say.

Whenever I get nervous, there's something I repeat to myself over and over.

Just hang on?

No. That doesn't work for me anymore. It works for some people, but not for me.

Then what?

You really want to hear it?

Yes.

You might think it's silly.

No, I won't. Why would you say that?

Okay, I'll tell you. It's very simple. It's just three little phrases. *Life is good. Be here now. Let it go.*

Life is good? Be here now? Let it go?

Yeah.

Where'd you hear that?

I read it in the *New Yorker* many years ago.

You don't look like the *New Yorker* type.

I'm not. Ronnie used to get it for the cartoons, and he'd leave the magazine lying around, and I'd flip through it to pass the time.

Ronnie who?

Ronnie Reagan, the late President.

You were a waiter during the Reagan administration?

Yeah.

Jesus, how old *are* you?

Not that old.

He starts to cough again, and Alan looks up at him, irritated. What the fuck is with that cough, Benny? Have you had it looked at?

It's nothing, Benny says. Something's going around.

"Something's going around!" Larry exclaims. I hate that fucking expression. What the fuck does it mean? There's always *something going around*. There's also shit going sideways and back and forth, but it doesn't mean a goddamn thing.

You should get your meds upped, Benny says.

Fuck you.

Christ! What happened to us? Michael says. We're supposed to be the Cool Table.

If I hear the expression "Something's going around" one more time, I will stick this fork in that person's ass. What are you so pissed off about?

Chuck said Courtney Love was doing the lecture today, and he swore on The Bible, and he was just fucking with me.

What's so great about Courtney Love?

If I have to explain it to you, you wouldn't understand.

I like her lead guitarist, that big tall blonde.

I hear she goes out with this little guy who is supposed to be some kind of genius writer or something.

I sit there shaking my head, wondering how I ended up in this place with all these crazy bastards.

Alan looks at me. I bet I know what you're thinking, he says. I bet you're asking yourself how you ended up at this place with all us crazy bastards.

That's not what I'm thinking at all! I lie. But it bothers me. How the fuck did he know? Am I that transparent?

Larry has gone off to get desert, and he's back now with a slab of apple pie. Guess who's doing the lecture today? he says.

Who?

Robert Downey Jr.

Liar.

I'm not lying, he says. Lorraine told me.

Who gives a shit?! I say. They all turn to look at me. What difference does it make? Do you guys really learn anything from watching these losers tell you their pathetic stories? Is it supposed to inspire us or something? Don't you get it?—they are Losers with a Capital L. You're not going to learn anything from them. You've got to do it for yourself! Without them! Without anyone!

Boy, you've really got a hair up your butt today, Jimmy.

No, Alan says. He's got *two* hairs up his butt. And I can hear them rubbing together. And pretty soon his ass is going to spit fire.

Fuck you guys, I say. If you want to spend the rest of your lives in Church Basements, whining, and, worse, listening to other people whine, then by all means— buy into the bullshit. But then you'll become addicted to *that*, and frankly, if I had to choose between that and a nice bottle of Pinot, it's No Contest.

That's harsh, Larry says.

If you don't like it here, Alan says, why don't you pick up what's left of your ear and leave?

I'm thinking about it, believe me. I don't want to be like you guys. I AM NOT A VICTIM. I AM NOT A VICTIM. I AM NOT A VICTIM.

I like your fire, kid, Benny says.

You know, he's got a point, Danny says.

You're right, says Larry. He does.

I wish you were wrong, though, Alan says. I'm weak, and I need this place, even the bullshit lectures.

I look up at the guys, and half of them—well Danny, anyway—are tearing up. What the fuck did I do? I told the truth, that's what I did, and these guys are fucking crying! This is worse than *American Idol*. This is like the *Miss America Pageant*.

I say, One day I'm going to write a book about this fucking place, and I'm not going to use your names— because I don't want to humiliate you guys, and because there's a very slight chance that some fact-checker might question me. And when you read my book, and you recognize yourself in the pages, and you're *honest* about what you see, maybe that will finally help you change.

Who the fuck are you? Tony Robbins?

I'm going to bigger than Tony Robbins. Not taller, but bigger.

I leave, and as I'm making my way down the corridor one of the Black Guys in White tells me that Lorraine wants to see me in her office.

When?

Now.

What does she want?

How the fuck should I know?

I go to Lorraine's office. You wanted to see me? I say.

Yes. Come in, Jimmy. Come in. The results of your test came back.

The Minnesota thing.

Yes.

How'd I do?

It's not like that. It's not about grades.

I know that. I'm not stupid. What did you find out about me?

You seem a little on edge, Jimmy. I hope this has nothing to do with Esther.

I realize this is a trick question, and I am impressed with the power of my own mind. Esther? I say. Who's Esther?

You might know her as Angelina. Esther is her real name.

Oh, of course! Angelina! I've seen her in the Mess Hall. Some of the guys think she's pretty hot.

But you don't?

No. She's not my type.

What is your type, Jimmy?

I'm not thinking about women at the moment. I'm just trying to get well.

Are you sure?

Why don't you ever believe me? You didn't believe me about Mort, and now you're giving me shit about Angelina.

Kudos. Good point, Jimmy, I apologize. But on the off-chance I'm wrong, please be careful. That old, adolescent fantasy—the whore with the heart of gold—is just that: a fantasy.

I get that she's calling Angelina a whore, and it kills me inside. And I want to punish her for it. But I can't Betray my True Feelings. She is watching me like a hawk, so I have to be cool.

I know that, I say.

You should get outside yourself more often, Jimmy. The world is a big place.

Is it? I think it's a small place, full of Small, Mean People.

I remember a funny line from Stephen Wright—*The world is a small place, but I wouldn't want to paint it*—and I bark like a seal.

You find this conversation amusing? Lorraine says.

No. I don't. Do you?

I'm not the one who's barking like a sea lion, Jimmy.

Sea lion? Well at least we've cleared that up. We haven't achieved Total Clarity, yet, but we're making solid progress.

I'm just going to say one more word on the Subject of Women, Lorraine says. Or maybe two words.

Everyone at Sleepy Hollow goes on at great length about everything, and then repeats it, belaboring it to death, I think. But it turns out I'm not *thinking* it; I've said it out loud.

It's the fresh country air, Lorraine says.

I think it's the nuclear facility on the other side of the river, I say. But that's just One Man's Opinion.

Jimmy, *focus*. The one thing I want to say is this: There will be plenty of girls lining up around the block for a handsome, sensitive, tough guy like you, but please wait until you have your life back. Are you listening to me? Wait until you have your life back.

Wait until.

Your Life.

Back.

You have.

Why has she turned into Yoda?

Okay, I say, and I glance at the clock, thinking about My Tryst, which remains hours away. You said my tests came back?

Yes. She glances at the papers on her desk, flipping through them, and reaches for her reading glasses. They're those little half-moon thingies, like Mrs. Murchison had in grade school, and suddenly I think Lorraine looks kind of hot. I've heard that intelligent women are better in bed, so maybe that's it. I wouldn't know, personally. No intelligent woman has ever gone to bed with me.

You're depressed, Lorraine says. And you have very little self-esteem. You're also quite insecure, and your insecurity makes you want to build yourself up.

Please don't stop! I say theatrically. I'm *loving* this!

Are you being sarcastic?

Thank you for noticing.

There are good things, too, Lorraine says.

Well can you get to them before what's left of my self-esteem seeps out of my asshole?

This really touched a nerve with you.

I drink Pinot Noir! I Dance! I am Garbage!

Lorraine slaps me hard. Snap out of it! she says.

I put my hand to my stinging cheek. I can't believe she just did that, but I don't blame her for it. I *was* out of control. I look at her with Grudging Respect, and I finally understand what that means.

I'm sorry, I say.

Everything is fine, Jimmy. You're a terrific guy. And I have every confidence that you are going to be among the fifteen percent who make it.

But?

But there was one Red Flag.

What?

You seem to have a tenuous grip on reality. You have a vivid imagination, which will doubtless serve you well as a writer—if you're thinking about writing fiction, and if you ever learn how to write a decent sentence—but it will get you in trouble if you're not careful.

My dream comes back to me. The bad part—Part Two. I know there was a message in there somewhere, but it feels almost out of my reach, like when you're reading one of those Mensa quizzes in an airplane magazine and you kind of think you know the answers but you get every single one of them wrong.

What are you saying? I ask Lorraine.

The *truth*, Jimmy. The truth is what matters.

I know that! I snap, sounding like a hurt adolescent. That's what I've been saying my whole life.

I know, Jimmy, she says, visibly exasperated. I know.

I get the feeling that she's suddenly given up on me. And it's a horrible feeling. It's like when you disappoint your father, and he turns to you and says, coldly,

"Okay, Jimmy. Do what you want. Go ahead. Do whatever you want." That's a terrible thing to say to a child. If you have a child, please never say that to them. And if you don't have a child, but you see someone saying it to their child, please ask them to stop. It is very damaging. It's like telling the child you don't really give a fuck.

Jimmy? Where'd you go?

Nowhere. I'm right here.

I seem to have lost you there for a moment. What were you thinking about?

I was thinking about Benny. I was thinking how much I like him, and what a great guy he is, and that it's too bad he never got married and had kids. He would have made a wonderful father.

Benny told you he never married and had kids?

Uh huh.

It's a lie, Jimmy.

It is?

Benny murdered his wife.

What?!

This is too much. This is amazing, but in a horrible way, and I don't want to hear it.

Well, technically, I can't call it murder, Lorraine says. He was acquitted. Mostly because the body was never found. But everyone knows about the wood-chipper.

He murdered his wife?! *My* Benny?!

Lorraine nods. He had two sons, she adds. Wonderful boys. They never forgave him.

What happened to them?

You don't want to know.

You're right! I don't!

I'll tell you anyway.

Why?!

Does the name Jim Jones mean anything to you?

No.

Guyana?

Isn't that some kind of fruit?

No. That's *guayaba*.

I tried a juice made from that fruit once. I wasn't impressed.

Focus, Jimmy.

I can't. I'm too upset. I don't want to hear this story about Benny. Benny is my friend. Benny would not lie to me. How do I know *you're* not lying to me? What is Truth, anyway? And are aspects of it fungible?

Benny is a sick man, Jimmy.

I said I didn't want to hear it!

I mean that literally. Haven't you been paying attention to that horrible cough?

No. Was I supposed to?

Benny is dying.

No! Don't say that!

I cover my ears and run out of the room, making loud noises to drown her out—and to kill kill kill the pain in my heart.

To

Kill

Kill

Kill

The

Pain

In

My Heart

By the time I get back to my room, I'm crying like a little girl.

Crying. Like. A little. Girl.

But I'm also thinking that that bit about killing the pain in my heart would make some kick-ass lyrics.

I wipe my tears and wonder, What is wrong with people? Why can't we be nice? Why can't we get along? Why is it that the best we can manage is enlightened self-interest? And what does that *mean*, anyway? That we just pretend to care about other people to get what we want from them? I can't believe that. If I believed that, I would think the world was a horrible place, and it's not. There's a lot of beauty out there. In nature. In art, too, though museums depress me. Why do we have to stick everything pretty in one place? How many paintings can you look at in an hour without feeling like you need a drink? And nature isn't all that great either, come to think of it. You see a beautiful shot of the Alaskan Wilderness, but they don't show you the black flies.

Focus, Jimmy, I tell myself. *Focus*.

Why would Benny lie to me? Why?

I pass out.

I come to.

I drink Pinot Noir. I Dance. I am Garbage.

No, I don't! That's all in the past.

I pass out again, and when I wake up, bathed in sweat, I realize I've missed lunch, and who knows what else, and that it's almost time to see Angelina. I pull myself together and shower and shave and brush my teeth twice. I cup my hand over my mouth and test my breath. It smells nice.

I climb out the window and I knock The Bible over by mistake, and it lands on the floor with a loud noise. For a moment, I wonder if that's some kind of Evil Omen. But I don't think so. It's not my Bible. They put it there. They put one in every room. And I Don't Believe, anyway.

I DON'T FUCKING BELIEVE.

If it was my Bible and I believed, I probably would see it as an Evil Omen, or at least a sign of some kind. And chances are I wouldn't go to the Clearing to have congress with Angelina, much as I wanted to. Because if I did, I could get Struck Dead, or, worse, Struck Limp.

God! I wish I hadn't thought that. Please don't let me have Performance Anxiety!

Please please please!

I hurry through the woods to our Clearing. Angelina is waiting for me on the blanket. My soul cries out like a Howitzer.

Thank God you're here! she says. I was worried that my message was too subtle.

No no, not at all! It was perfect. We understand each other perfectly.

I sit down next to her, and I notice that she hasn't shaved her legs. No matter.

I've been thinking about you, I say. I've been thinking about you incessantly. I know that in these situations it's wise to pretend you're not interested, but I want our relationship to be honest above all things.

That's sweet.

Did you miss me? I ask, because we seem to have reached some kind of conversational impasse.

Yes.

That's good, I say. *No one has ever missed me before. People tend to be happy when I'm gone.*

I'm beginning to see why, she says, but she's smiling, so I know she's kidding. I *think*.

She takes my left arm and kisses the wrist. Her lips are Soft. Tender. Gentle. I imagine them doing unspeakable things to other parts of my body.

Hey! There's that tattoo again.

Yes. I say. It's permanent.

Wait a minute? It says JIAL. Last time I looked, it looked like JAIL.

It's supposed to be Jail. Maybe you're not dyslexic when you're reading upside down.

Are you sure you were in jail?

Of course I'm not sure I was in jail! That tattoo doesn't have anything to do with jail! The letters stand for Jimmy Is A Loser. But I'm not going to tell her that.

I don't want to talk about the eighteen hellacious months I spent in Angola, I say. Eighteen months of savagery. Of watching my back, and my ass. Of fighting to protect my family name.

What were you in for?

It's a long story. There was this, uh—this mime.

A mime?

Yeah. One of those people who paint their faces and don't say anything and mimic people and call that Entertainment.

I know what a mime is. What happened with this mime?

He made sexual advances. Silently, of course. But it was obvious.

I don't know why I said mime! What the hell is wrong with me? No, I *do* know why I said it. I was in The Lounge two days earlier, and there was an old copy of *People* magazine in the trash, and I fished it out and read an article about a kid who beat a priest half-to-death for sexually assaulting him. But I didn't want to tell Angelina it was a priest just in case I'm wrong about God. I mean, if he does exist, he might choose this moment to strike me impotent—although I've always managed quite well without any help from him.

So you attacked him?

The mime? Yes. I beat him to within an inch of his life. Now I remember another reason I used a mime in the story. When I was fourteen, I went to the Metropolitan Museum of Art with my entire class, and there was this stupid mime there, and of all the kids he could have picked on, he picked on me. He mirrored everything I did. He walked like me. He turned his head like me. He put his hands in his pockets like me. He even cried like me. It was really fucking humiliating. I have hated mimes ever since.

But I don't understand, Angelina is saying. You were only protecting yourself.

Yes, I know, but his lawyers were very good. They kept saying, "Monsieur Levesque never said a word to him! He *never said a word*!" And of course it was true. The guy was a *mime,* for fuck's sake.

How horrible.

I am suddenly amazed by the way the mind works, my own mind in particular. First of all, it's astonishing that I would come up with such a brilliant defense for the mime on such short notice. Second, and perhaps even more significant, it might appear that I picked the name "Levesque" out of the air, but that name is in fact derived from *Le Vache*, which is French for priest, and hence I chose it for obvious reasons.

That's terrible, Angelina repeats.

But I'm not really listening. I'm trying not to think about the possibility that I might fail to achieve a satisfactory erection, so I find myself thinking about what Lorraine said about my tenuous grip on reality. Maybe she's right! Why I would make up such a stupid story? I was only in a jail once in my life, and they didn't even close the door to the cell. I was up in

Chappaqua, visiting my friends Harry and Sloane, or *former* friends, to be completely accurate, and I got pulled over for Driving Under the Influence. The cops were really nice. They got me a fresh pillow and let me lie on the cot until my father came to get me. And in the end they let me off with a warning.

Jimmy?

I snap out of it and tell Angelina that she looks really beautiful.

She kisses me. *Though it is the same as before, it isn't the same at all. It is more, stronger, weaker, deeper, quieter, louder. It is more, vulnerable, impenetrable, fragile, secure, unprotected, completely protected. It is more, open, deeper, full, simpler, true. It is more. True.* And don't ask me what the fuck I mean by that.

The next thing I know, we are ripping each other's clothes off, and trying to have sex. But it's not happening for me. Then she disappears in the general direction of my waist and does this really amazing thing with her lips—I can't see it but it involves loud, smacking noises—and Christ Almighty if it doesn't happen! I am home, people! I have arrived. A moment later, I am on top of Angelina and deep inside her Velvet Slipper.

And you know something. It Feels So Good! And it Feels So Right!

Feels

So

Good

And

Feels

So

Right

Then I am crying. And she's crying. And I'm trying to kiss away her tears, but she's looking around for her underwear.

We have to go, she says. We don't want to be missed.

You will never be alone, I tell her.

Can you pass me my shoe, she says.

Later, lying in bed, thinking of her, smelling her on my body, I realize I have fallen for her, and that I have fallen hard. Then there's a knock on the door.

Who is it?

Your mother's on the phone.

I go down the hall and pick up the phone.

Mom, I say. What's up?

I had a really strange dream. You were a guest on *Attika*.

That is so weird! I had the same dream!

I'm worried about you, Jimmy.

Why? Did something bad happen in the dream?

Not in the first part. The first part was great. Your father and I were in the audience, and we were so proud. I even dreamed that you bought the house in Costa Rica, that heavenly place near the Four Seasons, the one Dad and I rent every year for ten days, mostly to get away from you and your brother.

And then?

Then you were back on *Attika,* and she was very up-set about something.

What?

I don't know. I woke up crying. I was cry cry crying like a little girl.

I don't know what to say, Mom.

Is everything okay?

It's better than okay, Mom. Way better. I met someone.

Who?

A girl.

She's a patient there?

Yes.

I thought you weren't supposed to mingle with the women.

We're not mingling, Mom, and I say this with ambiguous intensity, hoping she'll guess what I mean.

Is she nice?

I think so.

Does she come from a good family? Are her parents in the Social Register?

I doubt it, Mom. I think she's one of the charity cases. There are always five or six of them—it helps Sleepy Hollow get Federal funding.

I can't wait to meet her, she says, but not very con-vincingly.

You will, Mom. And that's a promise. I think I love this girl. I *know* I love her, in fact, but I don't want to spell it out. That is so girlie.

Suddenly my mother is crying.

What's wrong? I ask her.

I don't know, Jimmy. All my life I've been preparing to let go of you, and in fact, ever since you were seven, and you freaked out about that silly little Bumper Car accident, when that kid broke his leg, part of me—a *big* part of me—has been looking forward to getting rid of you. But suddenly I don't know. You sound lucid for the first time in six years, and you're talking about being in love. It's really overwhelming.

I didn't mean to upset you, Mom.

No, no. Not at all. I'm very happy for you.

You should be, Mom. I'm back. We're going to be a Real Family again.

You sound like you're pretty crazy about this girl.

I am.

Remember when you were fifteen, she says, and I went through your wallet looking for drugs, and I found that old condom.

Yes, I do, I say tersely.

The thing had expired two years earlier! It was so dried out it was practically a fossil. But you still kept it. You still had hope!

What are you laughing about, Mom? I don't think it's that funny.

You don't remember this, but shortly after your mother abandoned you, and I moved in with your father, you decided you were going to welcome me into the family by crying and screaming like a lunatic.

I was two years old. I didn't *decide* anything. And I've heard this story a million times.

I thought you were just a cranky, ill-tempered little brute, determined to ruin everything for me and your father, so I would close the door to your bedroom and turn up Bizet's *Carmen*.

Until Maria insisted that you take me to the doctor! Jimmy?! You remember?!

No, Ma! Of course I don't remember. I was two years old!

The doctor said—

I *know* what the doctor said!

—"This boy is seriously constipated."

She's laughing so hard that she can hardly catch her breath. But I'm not laughing.

Okay, Mom. Enough.

"He's backed up all the way to the Long Island Expressway!" he said.

I know, Mom! And I am sick to death of this fucking story.

You know, Jimmy, she says sternly. Sometimes I wonder about you. Where's your sense of humor?

I'm sorry. It's been a long day. And I have another one of these goddamn lectures to go to.

Okay, fine!

She hangs up abruptly, like I did something to her. How come parents always do that?! How do they manage to turn everything around and make it your fault?

I hang up, upset. I can't understand why she thinks that story is so funny. I couldn't take a dump for six months. I was in excruciating pain. Where is the humor in that?

I make my way to the lecture, still fuming. There's a rumor it's going to be Kirstie Alley. I didn't know she drank and danced, and some fat guy I've never met tells me, She doesn't drink. But she eats. And there's a huge connection between dancing and drinking and eating and singing.

If there is, I can't see it.

It isn't Kirstie Alley. Big surprise! It's some weepy firefighter who was trying to pull a large woman from a burning building and dropped her. The woman weighed three hundred pounds, so I can see how the rumor about Kirstie Alley got started, but that's where the similarities end. The firefighter is crying.

She was heavy, yes, he is saying. And it was a bitch holding her up. And even if I was built like a brick shithouse, which I'm not, I would *still* have had trouble keeping a grip on her. But that's not the point. The point is, I'd been drinking. I was fucking drunk on the job. That woman died because I'd been drinking!

Now he's really sobbing. It's almost embarrassing. He pulls himself together, but barely, and he says, Here's the really sad part. The woman had the cutest little dog. And one of my colleagues had already got the dog out. And I could see the little dog down there, *way* down there, with his cute little doggy face, very expressive, looking up at us. And he looked genuinely worried, this dog. I don't know how else to put it. This dog understood that his mistress was in terrible danger, and it was really fucking him up. And then I dropped her, and Christ if she didn't land on the dog. Now the guy is falling apart. I mean, dry heaves and everything. I don't know where to look, but there are a couple of guys in the hall that aren't as sensitive as I am, and they're having trouble containing their laughter. Maybe they see the humor in a three hundred pound woman landing on the little dog that loves her beyond anything in the world, and being crushed to death, but I don't see any humor in it. I am not that type of person. I see the metaphorical value in a story like that—the *weight* of love and all, with the attendant responsibilities—but for me it's not a laughing matter. I don't want to cry, though. It seems all I do lately is cry.

The weepy firefighter pulls himself together, and we get into the question-and-answer part of the afternoon.

What kind of dog, was it?

I don't know. It looked like that little dog on *Frasier*.

A guy in the audience pipes up, That's a Jack Russell terrier. Great dog.

Why did you become a firefighter?

I don't know. I always liked playing with fire as a kid.

Do you have any pets of your own?

I have a Bearded Dragon.

What's that?

It's a kind of lizard.

Does it have a cute little expressive face?

No.

Is that why you got it?

I don't know. I never thought of that.

What are you doing now?

I'm trying to get my old job back.

I hope it's not in my home town, some guy says, and everyone cracks up.

Wow, I think. *People can be so cruel.*

As I file out, I see Benny, and I remember what Lorraine told me about how sick he is. I don't really want to talk to him because I'm not really comfortable around death and illness, and I go out of my way to avoid him. By the time I get to the corridor, he's long gone. I wonder what I'm going to do at dinner. I can't very well avoid him. Benny loves me like a son.

Later in the day, they have this stupid Graduation Ceremony, where Two Pathetic Guys are set loose on society again. There are a lot of speeches, and hugs, and crying, and one of the guys gets a Medal while the other one gets a Rock. I fall asleep before I can determine what this means, and frankly I don't give a shit. I'm in love and all I can think about is Angelina.

I decide to skip dinner that night, to avoid Benny. I go to my room and flip through *How to be Idiotically Happy.* One of the things the book says is that we expect too much from other people, and that this inevitably leads to disappointment. It says you should expect absolutely nothing from anyone, because that way you will *never* be disappointed. As you get better at this, you will expect so little from other people that you will feel good simply if you *make it through the day without getting the shit kicked out of you.*

I am amazed at how much sense this makes.

That night I sleep like a baby. I don't have any dreams, and I don't even get up to pee.

In the morning, I wake up and I can still smell Angelina on me, and the smell has gone a little sour by now, so I decide to take a shower.

When I go to breakfast, I see her, and I think she sees me, but she doesn't look at me for some reason, and I realize she is trying to be discreet. I look at her tray, and I notice a banana on the left, and a donut on the right, and this makes a perfect "10." So immediately I get it: I should meet her at the Clearing at ten. I am really excited. All that stuff about love's mysterious power, and the Ultimate Meaning of Life, and Finding Your Magical Missing Half—all of it is true and it is real and it is good.

I get to the table and Benny is not there, which is kind of a relief.

I ask Alan where he is, and he says, I don't know, but he was in the fucking tub for a fucking hour this morning, and he spent another hour shaving and trimming that jungle of hair in his nose, and he was singing.

Singing?

Yeah. You want me to spell it out for you. S-I-N-G-E-I-N-G.

Elliot makes a sound like a game-show buzzer. BWAAA! There's no E in singing, he says.

Fuck you.

That's weird, I say. And then I remember what Lorraine told me, about Benny being sick. Maybe he's getting cleaned up for his funeral, or is that someone else's job?

Guys, listen, I say finally. Is there anything to that rumor about Benny being sick?

Who told you that? Danny asks.

No one, I say. I just thought, you know, with all that coughing and everything, that there might be something wrong.

I think he's got The Big C, Larry says.

You think everyone's got The Big C.

You mean Cancer?

Give the boy a medal, Larry says.

Why do you have to be so unpleasant? I say.

I like it.

Guys, come on.

How's that little girlfriend of yours? Elliot says.

I don't know what you're talking about.

The women in this place, Michael says. They all look like they've been ridden hard and put away wet.

That's a really ugly expression, I say.

You know something, kid? Larry says. You're not half the man my mother used to be.

I take my tray and leave and find an empty table. I don't need those guys. I'm in love. "Top of the World, Ma!"

I finish breakfast in peace, but that ugly expression gnaws away at me. Much as I hate to admit it, Angelina *does* look like she's been ridden hard and put away wet. I want to introduce her to my parents, but I should probably get her cleaned up first. And I need to talk to her about those legs. Is there a subtle way to tell someone you love that you want them to shave?

While I'm sitting there, Larry comes by and drops a copy of *People* magazine on the table next to me. It's a familiar issue. It's the one I found in the trash, and *returned* to the trash.

There's a very interesting story in there, Larry says. About a kid who was molested by a priest, and almost killed him. He kicked him in the testicles repeatedly, *wanting* to kill him, but the priest lived, and the poor bastard kid ended up doing eighteen months in Angola. Wh-why are you telling me this? I ask, and I feel as if the world is closing in on me.

You know why, he says, and he laughs a crazy horror-movie laugh and walks away.

I wonder what the hell is going on here. I am very confused. How did he know about that story if he didn't hear it from Angelina? And why would Angelina tell him? And if Angelina told him, did he recognize it from the magazine? And who took the magazine out of the wastebasket? My head is spinning. I feel dizzy and weak and scared.

I look across at what used to be the Cool Table, but it has become the Asshole Table. Elliot and Michael start doing little mime things: you know, the exaggerated arm movements, the big surprised O with their lips, the bugged-out eyes. They start laughing uncontrollably.

When I go to put my tray away, Elliot and Michael sneak up behind me, startling me.

You should have killed that mime, Elliott says.

Yeah, Michael says. You let him live. See what happens when you spare a mime's life? They *talk*.

They think this is very funny, and once again they are doubled over with laughter, but I don't see the humor in it.

As I hurry back to my room, I can feel some of that old paranoia kicking back in, and I remember how hard it was on me, and on my father's secretary.

Just hold on, I tell myself.

Then I remember those three other phrases: *Life is good. Be here now. Let it go.* But they confuse me. What does it mean, *Life is good*. It doesn't feel very good to me right now. And why *Be here now*? Now is the last place I want to be. I feel like I'm losing my mind. And what is it I'm supposed to *let go* of? I wish Benny was here to explain it to me.

So I was never in Angola. Big fucking deal! Does that

make me a bad person? I don't think so. On the con-
trary, it makes me a *good* person.

I probably shouldn't have lied, though. But now that I
think of it maybe it's connected to my self-esteem.
Maybe that Minnesota test nailed it. About my insecurity and my low self-esteem and how I try to build
myself up. Man, I could sure use a glass of Pinot Noir.
I could use a fucking bottle, frankly.

What is wrong with me? Am I not interesting enough
as I am?

Fuck them. I'm not changing my story. And the stories are different, anyway. Mine is a *mime*; his was a
priest. How could you possibly confuse them? I mean,
in the history of the world, has there ever been a priest
who was also a mime? I don't think so. Is my story any
less believable than the story about the guy on the
Golden Gate Bridge who gets saved by the patrolman-
son he never knew he had? Again: I don't think so!
What matters is what YOU believe. FUCK ALL OF
YOU LOSERS! I KNOW WHO I AM!

I don't realize that I have screamed this at the top of
my voice, in the corridor, but I realize it now. Everyone is staring at me. I wave and smile, like I was just
making a little joke, and I hurry off to my room.

I Am A Man in Love.

A

Man

In

Love

I feel powerful. I strip and get in the shower and the water beats against me and it is hotter than a motherfucker. I reach over and adjust the temperature, and in a moment it is perfect, and I realize that *I* am perfect, too. Suddenly the whole world makes perfect sense to me. There is day, there is night. There is good, there is bad. The leaves fall of the trees, and the leaves jump back on the trees. Everything is as it should be, and we don't need to fight it, because *Life Just Is*. That's what makes it perfect. Left, right; up, down; cold, hot. It's like, you know, if you took a coin, and you said, This side is Good, and This side is Evil, you would always be worried about which side the coin was going to land on. But if you looked at the coin from *up above*, you would see that Good and Evil are *two sides of the same coin*, and You Would Understand Why It's Perfect. Or not. Of course, it's still a drag when the coin lands on the Evil Side, and the Asshole gets the Girl, but it's *less* of a drag because you understand it. And that's an amazing thing! It was for me, anyway. It was like I stepped out of the shower and there was this moment of Blinding Clarity and I finally understood The Meaning of Life. I felt *cleansed* in more ways than one. I felt as if I had been Wiped Clean of Illusion, Cleared the Fuck Out, and that this Metamorphosis was preparing me for The First Day of the Rest of My life. The First Day of the Rest of My Life!

Holy shit!

The

First

Day

Of

The

Rest

Of

My

Life

What a thought! Maybe I could put that on a T-shirt or something! Make millions!

I grab a fresh towel and dry myself, and cross toward the mirror. And then an incredible thing happens. *I want to see if I can face myself. I put my hands on the sink. They shake against the white porcelain. I start to look up toward the mirror. I can see my lips quivering. I get to my nose to the black lashes beneath my eyes I go to the bottom of my eyes. To the pale green. To the dirty green. To the green that is impure.*

All right! Enough! Just fucking *look* already!

I look.

I like what I see.

I like me.

I

Like

Me

I really truly like me!

I say it loud, screaming it at the top of my lungs, I LIKE ME!

I am giddy.

I get dressed.

I am going to see my Inamorata.

I climb out the window and run toward the narrow woods, with the wind blowing through my thinning hair.

I reach the Clearing, and there she is.

Fucking Benny.

He's grunting like a pig.

And he sees me and stops and looks up at me and smiles one of those Oh Shit! smiles.

Oh hey, kid, Benny says. I can explain.

But I don't want any goddamn explanation.

You killed me, Benny. You fucking killed me.

I am dead.

I am dead.

I used to drink Pinot Noir. I used to Dance. I used to be Garbage.

But now I am dead.

I am only dead.

Dead.

Dead.

Dead.

7.

I used to wonder why there were people like me in the world. Now I wonder why there are people like Benny in the world. And people like Angelina.

I run back, tears streaming down my cheeks, and I collapse near the Main Building. One of the Black Guys in White finds me and carries me to the infirmary, where I am sedated by the Kindly Nurse.

I slip into a deep sleep, and I dream.

I dream that I go home to my parents' magnificent Park Avenue co-op. And I make Amends. I ask them to forgive me for every horrible thing I've ever done to them, though there are more than we could possibly remember. We *do* spend a good portion of the evening enumerating some of my more egregious crimes, like the time I appeared naked at the top of the stairs, during a party at the co-op for the French Ambassador, and urinated on his wife's head.

In the dream, my parents take me with them to Costa Rica for the first time, to a palatial rental property on a cliff, with an infinity pool and views of the rainforest and the bay and the sparkling blue-green waters beyond (and room-service from the nearby Four Seasons).

My parents love this place, and now I love it, too. In my sobriety I realize that this is Heaven on Earth, and I would like to come down here often, so I ask my dad why he doesn't buy it, instead of just renting it for ten days every February.

Because I can't afford it, he says. You'd have to be seriously rich to buy this magnificent place.

But no matter. Every morning I sit at my computer, and I write. I write my story. An amazing story of pain and redemption. The story of a lost young man who finds his way back. Without help. Without God. A lost young man who does it On His Own, Who Does It His Way, and succeeds.

Finally, on the tenth day—and this is only a dream, of course—I write the last line in the book:

I'm ready. Yes, I'm ready.

I then take my book to my agent, because apparently my dream has supplied me with an agent, and I say, I've written a book about my life, and about my struggle with Pinot Noir and Dancing, but I don't want to hurt or embarrass anyone, so I want you to sell it as fiction. And she tries. God knows she tries! But the news is not good. The book is rejected seventeen times.

I am crushed, but suddenly I remember the story Benny told me—the bastard!—about a guy whose book was rejected seventeen times, a guy just like me, but he kept trying. He would not give up! He refused to be beaten! And I feel like I'm in the middle of one of those impossible novels where you never know where the fuck you are, because it's too hard to keep track of all of the goddamn characters, with all those similar sounding surnames, and because the fucking author is always showing off by jumping back and forth in time. But *this* particular novel, the one I'm in right now, turns out to be really fucking good. There are moments when you feel lost, certainly, *by design*, but by the time you get to the last page it all makes perfect sense. It makes so much sense, in fact, that it literally takes your breath away. The book is blindingly brilliant, a Masterpiece of Clarity, and it hits you with such force that you know *you have been changed forever*. Then suddenly it gets murky.

In my dream—I am still dreaming—the suggestion is made that we try to sell the book as a memoir. It is, after all, a memoir. And the only reason we were even trying to sell it as fiction was to Protect the Innocent. But what if I change a few more names, and a few obfuscating details, and resubmit it? It is an extraordinary story. Publishers need to know that it's a True Story. If they know that it's a True Story, they will see it with Fresh Eyes.

In my dream I try to see through the shadows. I try to identify this person who has made this brilliant suggestion, who has given me Hope. But I cannot see anything. Maybe I have only *myself* to thank? I don't honestly know. In an Earlier Dream, at that party, I squinted and tried to determine whether the Dominatrix really did have a curly little tail, like the Devil, or like a small, cute pig, but I couldn't see *that* either. So it's not as if I didn't layer in an excuse. There are things that are fated to remain unknown, and this is one of them. I know this now. And in some ways I am glad of it.

The first Publisher that gets the slightly revised book sees it with Fresh Eyes, as predicted, sees it for what it is, The Only Slightly Varnished Truth, and makes a decent offer. They have high hopes for the book. It is the extraordinary story of a Young Man Who Goes Through the Hell of Addiction. He drinks Pinot Noir. He Dances. And he feels like Garbage.

Who will not be moved by this beautiful book? the publisher asks.

I don't know, I say. Who?

It was a rhetorical question, my agent says, shushing me.

The book is published, and it languishes.

But then Attika reads it.

And she *loves* it.

And it takes the fuck off.

At-ti-ka!

At-ti-ka!

At-ti-ka!

Three million copies later, I wake up. Or am I still dreaming?

I buy the unaffordable house in Costa Rica.

I take the big room, with the panoramic views, and I let my parents have the other, smaller room, which is also very nice.

I love this place!

There are always lots of American Hotties at the pool at the Four Seasons, who are here to do some Serious Partying, and, during the off-season, there are more locals than you can shake a stick at.

I wake up in the infirmary.

Lorraine is standing over me.

This time I am definitely awake.

This is not a dream.

I repeat, This is not a dream.

Lorraine tells me that I have been out for three days.

What happened? I say.

You hit a rough patch, Jimmy, but you're back.

Angelina?

Gone?

Benny?

Gone.

I didn't dream that, then? The two of them, doing it in the Clearing?

No. I'm sorry. That was real.

I cry.

I cry like a little girl.

Like

A

Little

Girl

You're going to be fine, Lorraine says. Why don't you get washed up and come see me in my office.

I go back to my room and see that someone has left fresh flowers for me. I don't know whether this is a kind gesture or a sick joke. But just in case it's the latter I look at the flowers, hard, and I say, Fuck you!

I shower, then I go to see Lorraine.

I can't believe this happened, I say. I was in love with Angelina.

Angelina is trash, she says. I don't know why we let trash like that into the program.

I hear it helps get Federal funding.

That's true, she says.

Where is Angelina now?

I don't know. Last I heard, she and Benny made a scene in town.

What town?

That little one-street town where they took the lock off your ear.

I can picture the town. The grocery store, the hardware store, the coffee shop, the little shithole bar with a neon-sign in the window, and the barbershop. The doctor's office was above the barbershop, and that resonated for me at the time, and I find myself wondering, *again*, if that asshole was even a real doctor.

I wouldn't call that a town, I say.

Me neither, she says. But like a lot of small towns in this great country of ours, which is becoming increasingly polarized, and which is slowly but surely going to hell, there is a Trailer Park on the West Side. One of the trailers is a Crack Trailer, and that's where Angelina and Benny went first. The guy in charge was an Ugly Motherfucker, with half his face burned off from his previous job, in Meth production, and he felt bad that neither of them had any money. But because he had a Good Heart he told Angelina that he would give her a mid-size rock for a blow job.

That's horrible, I say.

You think that's horrible? Lorraine says. She blew him again so Benny could get high.

This is very painful to think about, I say. Any person who has ever been Betrayed in Love will doubtless share my pain.

I can make you forget her, Lorraine says, with some of that old ambiguity, and I look away, because I don't like the way she just crossed and uncrossed her legs. I don't want to go there. Instead, I think about the day my parents took me to Hawaii and paid a lot of money for me to swim with the dolphins. It was fun, and I felt a special connection to those big, smiley fish, but it doesn't really help me now. That was an innocent time, a time before I knew how shitty life could be, and remembering it doesn't do anything to Erase the Pain of Betrayal.

What are you thinking? Lorraine asks.

Not *you*, I want to say, but I have the wherewithal to understand that this would be unnecessarily cruel, and that she is not to blame, so instead I say, What the fuck do you think I'm thinking about?

Angelina?

Good guess, I say.

Calm down, Jimmy, she says. This is no time for The Fury to make an appearance. We know all about The Fury, and you've made your point, and it's time to put The Fury to bed.

You're right, I say.

And she is: From the point of view of this narrative, The Fury has served its purpose. It should be pretty clear by now that when someone gets in my face, I get them out of it.

You say that like you hate me, she says.

What the fuck does she want from me? I'm not going to sleep with her.

I don't hate you, I say. But I am a leaving this place.

You are not ready, Lorraine says.

When will I be ready?

When you can snatch the pebble from my hand, Grasshopper, it will be time for you to go.

What?

Nothing. That was before your time.

I am serious, I say. I am leaving.

I am serious, too. You are not ready. I do not see a Medal, and I do not see a Rock.

I do not need a fucking Medal, or a stinking Rock. And I do not need God, or inspiring lectures, or incomprehensible priests with warm, gentle eyes.

I know what this is about, she says. You are still in love with Angelina. And you still want her back. But

you can't save her, Jimmy. Do you hear me? You can't
save her!

This is not about her, I say. There is nothing here for
me. If I stay, what will I graduate to? Do you honestly
think I want to spend the rest of my life in Church
Basements, listening to a bunch of Losers talking
about the fact that their lives didn't turn out exactly as
planned. Hello! We are no longer swimming with
dolphins, people! It is time to wake up.

What was that about dolphins?

That's not the point! Life is hard, yes—but I am
harder.

That's not what I heard.

What are you insinuating? I say.

Nothing.

Yes you were! That was cruel and unnecessary.

It might seem cruel to you, now, Jimmy, but sometimes I have to take extreme measures to save someone. And I want to save you. I like you.

I like me, too. That's why I'm getting the hell out of
here. In this crazy world, nobody can save you but
you. That's what I believe, and I believe it with all my
heart. That is why I am leaving. Because I know that I
have to do this on my own.

Then I repeat, in a soft voice that is filled with pain
and longing, I have to do this on my own.

Lorraine is crying. A tear steals down her cheeks and
makes its way along erratically, in a serpentine pattern.
I want to thank you for everything you've done for

me, I say. And I thank you also for trying to talk me into staying, but my mind is made up.

Are you sure?

Yes.

She purses her lips and I think she is going to cry again, but she is strong.

I stand.

Can I have a hug? Lorraine asks me.

Sure, I say.

I give her a hug. She tries to wedge her thigh between my legs, but I don't let her.

Now I am walking along Main Street, or Only Street, as I prefer to call it. The Greyhound Bus is due in fifteen minutes, at noon, although it is seldom on time. The sun is hot and high in a clear sky. I hear the distant cry of a buzzard, and I say to myself, *I did not know there were buzzards in this part of the country.*

I walk into the bar to get away from the heat, but I am also there for another reason. A Hero's Journey involves many tests. Some of them take place in Grade School, and you hate them, and you cheat if you can, but others take place later in life, and you must face them like a man (or woman). Still other tests are self-imposed, and those are often the most critical. This is one such test.

I make my way toward the bar. The place is empty, except for the bartender, who looks up from his smallish newspaper as I approach. The headline says that Demi Moore and Ashton Kutcher have had a baby boy, and that they are going to name him Bruce. Truly, the world is a mysterious place!

Howdy, the bartender says.

Howdy, I say back, easing my tired buttocks onto a stool. You wouldn't happen to have a nice bottle of Beaux Freres? I ask.

Of *what*?

It's a very nice Pinot Noir. From the Willamette Valley.

Are you fucking kidding me?

How about a Rochioli then?

Say what?

That's a California Pinot. Also very nice. Russian River Valley.

I don't think so, pal.

Domaine Drouhin maybe? That's quite the wine, and a story goes with it. The French bought a spit o' land in the Willamette Valley, and they carried a bunch of grapes all the way across the Atlantic, and tried their luck on American soil. It paid off. It paid off big-time. Of course, now that I think about it, I'm not entirely sure they actually physically brought the grapes over from France. It's possible they used Oregon Pinot Noir clones, like Pommard or Wadenswill.

The bartender is looking at me like I'm a fucking lunatic.

Isn't it the Atlantic? I say. Wouldn't they have to cross the Atlantic? Or is it shorter the other way? I was never all that good with geography.

Do you want a drink or not, pal?

Yes I do. *Not.*

Excuse me?

Give me a shot off the Jack Daniel's.

He reaches for a shot glass, but I tell him I want a really Big Shot; a ten-dollar shot. So he fills a tumbler and slides it across the bar and a little spills over the side of the glass, like you see in movies. (Every fucking time!)

I reach into my pocket and put ten dollars on the bar, and he's still looking at me, so I put another dollar and half next to it. My father always said you should leave a good tip, but not so good that they want to follow you home, and I have lived by those wise words. I know a great many people who tip more generously than I do, but I think those people are simply insecure and want to be liked, even if it's only by an Italian waiter who is wearing so much cheap cologne that it ruins the entire dining experience.

Now I look at the Jack. I put my nose close to the Jack. I inhale the Jack's fumes, and for a moment I am reminded of a guy in college, a guy called Jack, who didn't bathe regularly.

But I blink and Smelly Jack is gone. Man, if only real life was like that!

You just get out of The Hollow?

I look up at the bartender. I like the way he said that, *The Hollow.* I wish I had thought of that. It sounds cool.

Yes, I say.

Everyone of you fucking guys comes in here, and

everyone of you fucking guys does exactly that same thing.

What? They ask for Monster Pinots that one would be highly unlikely to find in a seedy dive like this?

No, asshole. They come in. They order a drink. They look at it for a while and tell themselves that they are bigger and stronger than any lousy drink, then they leave and get on the bus. And just before the bus pulls away, they run back in and ask for a to-go cup.

That's not going to happen with me.

We'll see.

The bus pulls up, right on cue.

I look at the Jack. I am tempted, and for a moment my right hand almost betrays me. But I get the shaking under control, slip off the stool, tip my imaginary Stetson in the bartender's general direction, and walk out. I wish I was wearing boots, not Nikes. They would sound a lot cooler on the wooden floor. As it is, the floor has a nice creak to it.

I go outside. The bus doors open with a pneumatic hiss. I get on. I do not think about the Jack.

Do not.

I
Do
Not
Think
About
the
Jack

I think about that bartender, though, and about his lack of compassion.

Just as the driver is about to pull out, I say, Can you give me ten seconds please?

The driver rolls his eyes, like he's seen this before, and I know what he's thinking. But he's wrong. He couldn't be more wrong.

I walk into the bar, breathless, and the bartender grins a big, shit-eating grin. He thinks he knows why I'm there, but he's as wrong as the bus driver. Or wronger. Or equally wrong.

You know, I say. You are an asshole. There are a lot of people who aren't as strong as I am, and they will struggle with their addiction for the rest of their lives. They need God, and they need their Church Basements, and they need Buddies they can call in the middle of the night, even if it's just to hear themselves talk. Because that's the way it is sometimes. We are all people here. We all long for human connection.

What is your fucking point, asshole? he says.

My point is this: You need to be a more compassionate person.

That's what my ex-wife said, and you know what I told her? I've been lying to you all these years, bitch. You look fat in all your pants, and you look *really* fat naked.

I shake my head. This guy is beyond hope.

As I get back on the bus, I wonder why the world is like that. I remember the many lectures I was forced to attend, back at The Hollow, and I think in particular about that dumpy guy whose father was hit by a garbage truck. I bet his father was probably a nice man, and he probably didn't deserve that, but this bartender is a Total Asshole—and he's *alive*. Does that make any sense to you? Where's the Justice there? If this not the perfect argument against the Existence of God, I don't know what is.

I get home. My parents are not expecting me, but they act like they're happy to see me. I tell them that I have lived through a Truly Harrowing Experience, and that I'm going to write a book about it, and that they have nothing to worry about. The worst is behind me. I do not drink Pinot Noir. I do not Dance. And I no longer feel like Garbage.

I work on my book every day, and some days the words come clean and hard and true. But other days, nothing happens.

In February, my parents invite me, somewhat reluctantly, to go with them to the beautiful house in Costa Rica, which I've only ever seen during my father's mandatory, bi-annual slide-shows, and I fall in love with the place. It is everything they said it was, and more.

I write every day. And I keep writing. And the writing goes so well that I ask my father to please rent the house for another two weeks so that I can finish my book. This is a lot of money—somewhere in the neighborhood of twenty-eight thousand U.S. dollars—but my

father is so impressed with my sobriety that he says yes.
I write hard. Sometimes I walk over to the pool at the
Four Seasons, and I try to pick up American girls. I tell
them I'm a writer, and they ask me what I've written,
and I say, Nothing, yet. But I'm working on a novel.
They laugh. I get the impression they think I'm a nerd.
I settle for some of the local girls, who jack up their
prices because I'm an American.

Finally, I finish the book. When I go back to New
York, *everything happens just like in the dream!*

At first, the book gets rejected, and I start thinking
about Pinot Noir and Dancing, but I don't want to be
Garbage again, so I tell myself, *Just hold on!*

Just

Hold

On

One day, about twelve or thirteen rejections into the
process, the phone rings at my parents' co-op. My parents are not home, and Consuelo is in the shower,
thank God, so I answer it.

Hello?

Jimmy? Is that you?

Angelina?

Please don't hang up.

I don't say anything.

Jimmy, are you still there?

Yes.

Do you hate me?

No, I say. But I'm thinking, *Part of me does*.

I'm sorry, Jimmy. I know I hurt you.

Why, Angelina? Why would you do a terrible thing like that? After I told you that I would always be there for you and everything?

I don't know. I'm always sabotaging myself. I can't help it. And I felt really bad for Benny. He was dying.

I bet that was bullshit, too, I say.

No, Jimmy. That's why I'm calling. I just left the hospital. Benny's dead.

That's terrible, I say.

And I feel terrible. All the wonderful moments I shared with Benny barrel toward me, sort of like a montage. They were brief, but they touched me in a deep place, and when I think about them I almost cry like a little girl.

I

Almost

Cry

Like

A little

Girl

I am so alone, Angelina says. Will you come and see me?

Where are you?

Uptown.

You've been in New York all this time?

Yes.

Why didn't you guys call me?

We didn't think you wanted to hear from us.

I think about this and say, You're right. I didn't.

Please say you'll come, Jimmy. You are all I have.

I think, *Man, if I am all she has, she is in seriously deep shit*, but all I say is, Okay.

For a moment, I feel like one of those Abused Women who always keep going back for more, even when she knows her Bastard Husband isn't ever going to change, but then I realize that this is how love works. It has never made any sense, and it never will make any sense, but it beats this horrible, soul-crushing loneliness that seems to be the norm among people who have had at least two years of college.

She gives me the address, I write it down, and I leave the co-op.

I walk over to Madison Avenue, to a flower shop, and I use my father's Platinum American Express card to buy flowers for Angelina. I know I'm only supposed to use it in emergencies, but this seems to qualify. And it kind of pisses me of that he wouldn't give me that special Black Card with the million-dollar limit, because it shows that he doesn't really trust me.

I hail a cab and I notice that the driver is wearing a turban. I remember another turban, a lifetime ago, and I wonder if this is the end of my journey somehow. But no. This guy is a Sikh, and he was born in Cleveland, and he doesn't know any foreign languages.

Man, he says. That is *way* Uptown. I hate that part of town.

As we drive along, I see a Really Fat Lady on the street, and I think about the Fireman who dropped that 300-pound woman on her cute, expressive little dog, and I can't help myself: I laugh my little pinniped laugh.

The driver is right. The place *is* way Uptown. It is in a part of town that has never been gentrified and does not stand a chance in hell of ever being gentrified. He stops across the street from a real flea-bag, and I can see that something appears to be going on. There are two police cars and an ambulance out front.

Are you sure this is the right place? I ask Mr. Sikh.

Yes, he says. That's it across the street. I can't get any closer.

I thank him and pay him and get out and he takes off fast, his tires squealing.

People turn to look.

There are a lot of African Americans around, but I am not scared. I am not even scared when I realize I am the only White Guy around for miles, or as far as the eye can see, anyway, and that some of these people are looking at me like they have never seen a White Guy in their lives.

I move closer to the flea-bag, trying to work my way through the crowd, and I realize I must look a little stupid with a bouquet of fresh-cut flowers in my hand. I want to tell these nice people that I paid for them with a credit card, my *father's* credit card, and that I have hardly any cash on me at all, so I begin to think about ways I might be able to slip that into the conversation.

When I get to within view of the flea-bag, I turn to a handsome young man who's wearing a do-rag and a skimpy tank-top.

What's going on? I say. I try to sound cool. *Wuz goin' on.* And after I say it I realize that *down* would have worked better than *on*: *Wuz goin' down.*

Some White Crack Ho hung herself, he says.

I know it can't be Angelina, but a moment later I see them bringing someone out of the place, on a stretcher, under a ratty blanket, and my heart almost stops. As they negotiate their way down the stoop, the blanket slips a little and I catch a glimpse of leg. She still hasn't shaved. She looks like fucking King Kong.

I give the flowers to a Kindly Looking Black Lady, and then I go look for a cab. It takes me a really long time to find a cab in this part of town, and there are a few moments when I actually fear for my life, and when I wish I actually *knew* Krav Maga, even if it was only a few basic moves. Finally, an Older Black Man in a beat-to-shit DeSoto pulls up and offers to drive me home for a hundred dollars. I don't even try to Presbyterian him down.

On the way back to Park Avenue, I try to figure out how I feel about Angelina's death. It is painful, certainly, but in many ways I am relieved. I understand why she killed herself. She betrayed me, and she knew in her heart that she would have to live with that for the rest of her life. If we had somehow managed to patch things up, and got our own co-op, and had kids, that betrayal would not have gone away. Whenever we would argue—whether it was about the kids, or about the fact that the house was a mess, or about her refusal to even *try* to make a simple, home-cooked meal for me—there was a better-than-even chance that I would throw it in her face.

You fucked Benny! I would scream, and I wouldn't care if the kids were in the room. You fucked Benny, you bitch!

She would run from the room, crying, and she might say something like, Are you ever going to let that go! You are fifty-two years old, for Christ's sake! When are you going to let it go!

And I would follow her, all red in the face, still shouting, No! I am never going to let it go. When I'm on my fucking death bed, I will make sure that those are my last words to you. YOU FUCKED BENNY!

By this time she would be cowering on the bed, sobbing, trying to cover her head with a pillow, and I would move in real close. I would pretend I was a dying man, and I'd get right in her face, and in a very low voice, my words barely audible, and with each word getting progressively fainter, I would say, You. Fucked. Benny.

Then I would do an imitation of a death rattle, and laugh my little pinniped laugh.

So you see, if you think about it, Angelina hanging herself is the right ending. I won't say it is a Happy Ending, because it isn't, and that would be misleading, but in some ways it is the Perfect Ending, and that's good enough for me.

When I get back from this horrible part of town, a part of town I never even knew existed, I wonder if I should tell my parents about Angelina, but they are there with Janos, their Hungarian friend from Caracas, so I don't bother them. Plus they never met her. Why would they care? They have their own lives, even if those lives are alarmingly shallow.

Two weeks later, my agent calls to tell me that my book has been rejected yet again, for the seventeenth time, and she invites me to have a drink.

Coffee! she says, correcting herself. I meant *coffee*.

A few days later I stop by her office, just as she's wrapping things up, and we're all sitting around: my agent, Several Unidentified Assistants, a Secretary, members of the Cleaning Crew, a guy from FedEx, et cetera, when someone—I don't know who exactly—comes up with the idea of selling the book as a so-called *recovery memoir*. Just like in the dream! As we discuss it, we realize, *collectively*, that this is a relatively easy fix, because that had always been the Original Intent. So it takes almost no rewriting at all, which is good—because frankly, by this time, I am so sick of the book I don't even want to look at it.

And just like in the dream, a publisher bites. And the book is published. And it languishes.

Until At-ti-ka puts me on her show.

And then it takes the fuck off.

My God! I had no idea there was this kind of money to be made in publishing! If I had known, I would have gotten into writing much sooner. I would urge anyone with even a soupçon of talent to get into it. It's not that hard.

As the checks being rolling in, big honking checks, I realize that I need to do something with my money. And one of the first things I do is to buy the place in Costa Rica.

My parents keep bugging me to visit, so I let them fly down for a week. My father argues that they should get a full ten days, like they used to, saying that I would never even have known about Costa Rica if it wasn't for them, and I see his point and toss in an extra night (but they have to be out by 11 a.m. the following morning.)

On their last morning there, we are in the kitchen, and they are packed, and all the good things that have happened to me make me feel incredibly powerful. I see a banana on the counter and I hold it in my hands and close my eyes and focus.

What are you doing? my father asks.

Nothing, I say.

But that isn't entirely true. I was trying to see if I could turn one banana into several bananas, like Jesus allegedly did (if he even existed!).

After my parents leave, I go over to the Four Seasons pool and it is crawling with Hot Babes. They all know who I am, and they like me for reasons which are only too obvious. But so what? That's one of the perks of success. Women aren't stupid. I don't blame them for not liking me when I was a nerd who was still being supported by his father, and who only *said* he was writing a book.

I invite two of the girls to come over later, saying I have to go back to work on my new book, *My Friend Benny*, but to come by at five o'clock for cocktails. I myself don't drink, but I keep plenty of booze around for Less Enlightened people. They giggle girlishly and say they will see me at five.

I can't wait, one of them says.

Me neither, says the other.

I can see I'm in for a very stimulating evening, intellectually speaking.

I go back to My House and write for a while, but after about eight or nine minutes I get tired. This book isn't moving as quickly as my first book, and I am having trouble with some of Benny's bullshit. On the other hand, I guess it's okay to say that Benny was with Covert Ops, because that's what I *thought*, but it still doesn't track properly. And how am I going to handle the whole betrayal thing with Angelina? How does that make *me* look? Like a schmuck, right?

All the hard thinking tires me out, and I take a nap.

I have a terrible dream.

I dream that I am still getting interview requests, even though I've begged off because I need to focus on my

new book, and that a couple of very persistent re-
porters are beginning to ask some pretty embarrassing
questions. I try to answer them as well as I can, but I
am worried, so I call my agent, and my publisher, to
express my concern. Or maybe not. Maybe in the
dream I only *think* about making the calls.

But whatever I did or didn't do, in the dream I once
again find myself on *Attika*, and Attika is pissed. So are
the women in the audience. Frankly, they are *beyond*
pissed. There is one scrappy looking wench in the
front row who looks so pissed that I find myself hoping that Attika's security crew is as professional and ef-
fective as those big, stupid thugs on *Jerry Springer*.

Attika says, You lied to me! You lied to everyone who
read your book! You lied to everyone who turned to it
for inspiration! What do you have to say for yourself?

I don't say anything. I can't say anything. Because I
am crying.

I am crying.

Cry cry crying.

Like. A little. Girl.

Attika turns her fiery gaze on Muffy Talons, my
publisher.

What responsibility do you take for this? she says, her
voice cold as steel.

And Muffy Talons says, in that little rich-person voice
of hers, I read the manuscript as a memoir. It was an
extraordinary story.

Didn't you check the facts?!

We just don't have the manpower for that kind of thing, Muffy says. And I believed his story. It rang true. I myself had both of my ears pierced, when I was twelve, and it hurt like a motherfucker.

The audience gasps. That last word gets bleeped out for the people at home, but when you're there, live, you hear it. You. Hear It.

Attika turns toward me. How many millions did you make off this lie? she asks.

Boy! She is really determined to extract her pound of flesh, isn't she? What is wrong with her? Hasn't she ever heard of *symbolism*? Does she even know what a *metaphor* is?

I don't know how much, I say. A lot of money, I guess. I know *exactly* how much I made, and it *is* a lot of money. In fact, it's way more than anyone even thinks it is. The advance was fairly modest, so my genius agent negotiated a hell of a deal on the back end. The fact is, I don't have to worry about money for the rest of my life. How great is that?

Attika asks me another question: The mime? Was that true?

The mime? I say. I have no fucking idea what she's talking about. The only mime I can remember is the one who humiliated me at the Met when I was a kid, and I'm still pissed off about it. He's the reason I have never in my life gone back to an art museum, and as a result can't really tell the difference between a Corot

and a Cézanne. Did I even have a mime in my book?
And *why*?

I asked you a question, Jimmy?

I ASKED YOU A QUESTION!!!

I wake up in a sweat.

Holy shit!

That was intense.

For a moment there, Attika had turned into the Devil.

But it was only a dream. A horrible dream.

A

Horrible

Silly

Dream

It was not a Dancer Dream.

And it was not a Writer Dream.

It was a Bullshitter Dream.

But so what?

That's the way the world works, people!

Wake the fuck up.

It's *all* bullshit, you most of all.

Yeah, *you*.

And I know what you think. You think this is cyni-
cism talking. You think I'm being cynical because my
monthly bank statement tells me that I can *afford* to be
cynical. Or, indeed, that I can afford to be ANY-
THING I FUCKING WELL WANT TO BE!

No! *This* is the truth.

Because the time has come, people.

You know what I say?

I say, Fuck The Bullshit It's Time To Throw Down.
(FTBITTTD!)

The world is a horrible place.

People are horrible.

And *you* are especially horrible.

Fucking Loser!

But not me, baby.

No, not me.

I am not a loser.

I'm a Big Winner.

I have a co-op in Manhattan, I have this unbelievable house in Paradise, and I have Enough Money to Last Me the Rest of My Life.

God, I love this place.

This is where I finished my book.

Right there.

I remember sitting at that desk, and writing the last line:

I'm ready. Yes, I'm ready.

I cry.

I cry cry cry.

I cry like a little girl.

Like

A

Little

Girl

Then I snap out of it and wipe my tears.

That all happened a long time ago.

A long, long time ago.

I look out the window.

I see the two girls from the Four Seasons coming up
the long, steep drive.
They are coming to see me.
And man, they look hot!
I bet I'm going to do them both tonight.
Isn't it pretty to think so?

acknowledgments

Our thanks to the team at ReganBooks—Judith Regan,
Michael Broussard, and Cassie Jones—for giving us a
whole week to write this book.